Djeha,
the North African Trickster

Djeha,

the North

African

Trickster

Edited by

Christa C. Jones

University Press of Mississippi / Jackson

The University Press of Mississippi is the scholarly publishing agency of
the Mississippi Institutions of Higher Learning: Alcorn State University,
Delta State University, Jackson State University, Mississippi State University,
Mississippi University for Women, Mississippi Valley State University,
University of Mississippi, and University of Southern Mississippi.

www.upress.state.ms.us

The University Press of Mississippi is a member
of the Association of University Presses.

First printing 2023
∞

Library of Congress Cataloging-in-Publication Data

Names: Jones, Christa, editor.
Title: Djeha, the North African trickster / Christa C. Jones.
Description: Jackson : University Press of Mississippi, 2023. | Includes
bibliographical references and index.
Identifiers: LCCN 2023016708 (print) | LCCN 2023016709 (ebook) | ISBN
9781496847041 (hardcover) | ISBN 9781496847058 (trade paperback) |ISBN
9781496847065 (epub) | ISBN 9781496847072 (epub) | ISBN
9781496847089
(pdf) | ISBN 9781496847096 (pdf)
Subjects: LCSH: Berbers—Africa, North—Folklore. | Folklore—Africa,
North. | Tales—Africa, North. | Kabyles—Folklore. | Berbers—Folklore.
| Tricksters—Folklore. | Algeria—Folklore.
Classification: LCC GR353.2.B43 D54 2023 (print) | LCC GR353.2.B43
(ebook) | DDC 398.20961—dc23/eng/20230522
LC record available at https://lccn.loc.gov/2023016708
LC ebook record available at https://lccn.loc.gov/2023016709

British Library Cataloging-in-Publication Data available

Contents

Acknowledgments

I am most grateful to Mary Heath, associate editor, and Katie E. Keene, editor-in-chief at University Press of Mississippi for their guidance, for their encouragement, and for moving this book toward publication. In particular, I would like to thank Kelly Burch, copyeditor; Corley Longmire, associate project editor; and Joey Brown and the marketing team at the University Press of Mississippi for their hard work. I am very grateful for the comments made by the two anonymous readers commissioned by the press, and I would also like to thank administrators at Utah State University, in particular former department head Bradford Hall, former executive vice-president and provost Francis D. Galey, associate vice-provost Janis Boettinger, and Dean Joseph ("Joe") P. Ward, for granting me a research leave during the academic year 2021/22. I am grateful to my colleagues Abdulkafi Albirini and Asmaa Yasidi Alaoui for their help with transliteration of Arabic and Berber terms. Last but not least, I give a big shout-out to my daughter, Audrey Annie, for her insightful remarks and to my trickster husband, Brett Travis Jones, for his editorial input and his unfaltering support.

Note from the Editor and Translator

Auguste Mouliéras's 1892 trickster collection *Les Fourberies de Si Djeh'a* (*Si Djeh'a the Schemer*) contains sixty folktales about the trickster's daily life and his interactions with the villagers and various individuals he encounters. These sixty tales are numbered and titled but, for the most part, they are thematically unrelated and chronologically disconnected, with the exception of a few tales dealing with the prankster's wife (chapter 1), his students (chapter 5), thieves (chapter 5), and the numerous folktales centered on foodways (chapter 4). In some tales, the trickster protagonist is young and gullible, while in others, he is either married and shrewd or old and cunning. To enhance the reading experience and provide context about French Algeria and Berber culture, each chapter is preceded by a short introduction, while the tales are arranged thematically. Each of the six chapters contains ten folktales revolving around a common theme: "Family and Kinship" (chapter 1), "Animal Tales" (chapter 2), "Faces, Places, or Daily Life in the Village" (chapter 3), "Foodways" (chapter 4), "The Intricacies of Hospitality: Beware of Friends and Foes!" (chapter 5), and "Religion, Death, and the Afterlife" (chapter 6). This themed structure is intended to help general

readers navigate the Djeha folktale maze, while the intro-
ductions provide historical and cultural information about
French Algeria and Berber culture that might be unfamiliar
to Anglophone readers. Mouliéras's translation is somewhat
dry and repetitive. It paradoxically often lacks humor. In my
modern translation, I have tried to do justice to the humorous aspect of the jocular tales and anecdotes. Mouliéras's
stilted rendition might be in part attributable to the ver-
tical mode of transmission of the tales and the different
personalities of his various informants. He collected the
tales from members of the Beni Jennad El-Bahar tribe, who
worked as masseurs, and from one person called Amor
Ben Mohammed Ben Ali, a member of the Beni Jennad
El-Bahar tribe (see "Introduction").

When reading the tales, it emerges that some clearly
originate from the same informant while others are sty-
listically very different. Many are short and snappy, while
others are long, windy, and repetitive. More than a century
later, it is difficult to comment on the exact nature of the
relationship between Mouliéras and his various informants,
including Amor Ben Mohammed Ben Ali (see Mouliéras
1893, I) whom he credits as his main informant. Were they
acquaintances, friends, or did Amor Ben Mohammed
Ben Ali consider Mouliéras a figure of authority? Equally
important, it should be noted that these trickster folktales
were primarily orally transmitted for many centuries and
not meant to be read in book form in the first place.[1] They
were foremost oral, communally told folktales, and each
storyteller had their own personal storytelling style, repertoire, and unique storytelling skills. Some storytellers
had undoubtedly more incisive storytelling techniques
or better punchlines than others. Jean Déjeux's bilingual

(Berber-French) edition *Les Fourberies de Si Djeh'a: Contes kabyles* (1987) is a verbatim reedition of Mouliéras's book. In my English translation, I have attempted to—whenever possible—bring out the punchline of the trickster's jokes, jests, or pranks.

Djeha,
the North
African
Trickster

Tracing the Trickster in North African Folktales

This collection of jocular trickster folktales, pranks, jests, and anecdotes is a translation of Auguste Mouliéras's *Les Fourberies de Si Djeh'a* (1892; *Si Djeh'a the Schemer*). It was first published in the Berber Zwawa dialect in 1891, followed by a bilingual French-Berber edition by Mouliéras in 1892, which is the basis for this translation. *Djeha, the North African Trickster* revisits Mouliéras's sixty folktales that star an enduringly popular folktale character called Djeha. This iconic figure is the Maghrebian trickster par excellence (Galley and Iraqui Sinaceur 1994, 51).[1] He is, in fact, the "most popular protagonist of jocular tales, jokes and pranks in the Arab world" (Marzolph 2017, 139). In the northern Algerian mountain range of Kabylia, which provides the setting for this folktale collection, Djeha is a quintessential figure, an "imaginary character with whom the Kabyles like to identify" (Bourdieu 1979, 15), probably due to the trickster's proverbial cleverness, stubbornness, and disrespect for figures of authority. We will see that the North African Djeha (also sometimes spelled Djoha, Juḥā, or Ǧuḥā) in this collection is poor, hungry, clever, cunning, and resourceful. He plays pranks on the rich and powerful out of necessity, usually to find something to eat and to survive. Djeha is a rebellious, nonconformist, and free agent at a time when Algeria was a French colony (1830–1962). The Kabyle tribes were colonized by the French from 1851 to 1857 (so roughly, three decades after the conquest of Algiers in 1830), with insurrections against the French occupant occurring in the Aurès mountains in 1859 and in Hodna in 1860. Finally, a major revolt occurred in Kabylia in 1870 that was crushed, marking the end of colonization of Algeria by the French (Lacoste [1995] 2004, 28).

The Origins of Djeha/Juḥā and His Twin Brother Nasreddin Hoca

The historical origins of the Djeha figure are extremely varied and complex. The longevity and geographical diffusion of this hybrid and migratory character that is rooted in oral tradition and that has evolved tremendously over a very long period of time explain why he is anything but a uniform or static character.[2] As Islamicist philologist, folklorist, and Ǧuḥā scholar Ulrich Marzolph notes:

First, it is important to keep in mind that Ǧuḥā, as he is known and perceived toward the end of the twentieth century, *is a popular jocular character whose image developed over a period of more than a thousand years.* It was a long way from the first mention of Ǧuḥā in the poetry of ʿUmar b. Abī Rabīʿa, who died around the year 93/712, to the vigorous

component of oral tradition in the Arab world that
he represents today. (1992, 164; emphasis mine)

In *Medieval Islamic Civilization: An Encyclopedia*, Marzolph
examines the trickster's origins, lists various manuscripts,
and notes that the modern Djeha figure—the one depicted
in the folktales in this collection—has been fashioned by
traditional Arabic narratives, folktales of the Turkish jester
Nasreddin Hoca, and nineteenth-century print tradition:

Juha [*sic*], a pseudohistorical character, is the most
prominent protagonist of jocular prose narratives in
the entire Islamic world. The first securely datable
anecdote about Juha is narrated in both al-Jahiz's
(d. ca. 255 AH/869 CE) *al-Qawl fi l-Bighal* (*Remarks
About Mules*) and his *Rasa'il* (*Epistles*). Substantial
anecdotal material about Juha is available in the
large adab[3] compilations of the tenth and eleventh centuries, such as the works of al-Tawhidi (d.
414/1023) and al-Abi (d. 421/1030). By the eleventh
century, Juha had already been firmly established as
a "focusee" of a cycle of jocular prose narratives, and
a booklet devoted to these narratives is listed in Ibn
al-Nadim's *Fihrist* (*The Index*; a late tenth-century
Baghdad bookseller's bibliography of works he knew
or believed to be extant). During the following centuries, the character attracted ever more material.
The only monograph collection of his tales surviving
from premodern Arabic literature, a booklet called
Irshad Man Naha ila Nawadir Juha (*The Guidance of
Those Who Feel Inclined to the Stories of Juha*), was
compiled by Yusuf ibn al-Wakil al-Milawi in the

seventeenth century and contains a total of seventy-four tales. The modern image of Juha was shaped by nineteenth-century print tradition. Printed editions of Juha's tales present an amalgam of traditional Arabic material about him, together with tales that had originally been attributed to the Turkish jester Nasreddin Hodja [sic] and anecdotes derived from traditional Arabic literature. (2006, 426; emphasis mine)

It is indeed important to point out that the Berber prankster Juḥā, or Djeha—as he is called in France and in this collection—has a famous twin brother called Nasreddin Hoca in modern Turkish. Hundreds of Nasreddin aphorisms and tales circulate all over the Arab and Islamic worlds, from North Africa via the Balkan region and the Middle East (including Iran) to Middle, and South Asia. Nasreddin Hoca, who might have been a real person,[4] probably goes back to the thirteenth or fourteenth century:

Some of the most wide-reaching examples of the impact of traditional jocular tales in the Muslim world are the jokes and anecdotes attached to the character of Nasreddin (Başgöz and Boratav 1998; Marzolph 2006). *Whether or not a person by this name, obviously a minor cleric, ever lived in Anatolia in the thirteenth or fourteenth century is a question of historical relevance that fades into insignificance considering the characters spread all over the Muslim world.* Today, we witness an all-encompassing reception of the Nasreddin-tales literally "in the footsteps of the Prophet Muhammad," i.e., in every language and culture that was or still is influenced by Islam, from Sephardic Spain[5] to Uyghur culture in Communist China. Considering the syncretistic nature of popular tradition, Nasreddin over the centuries has incorporated the narrative repertoire of numerous other jocular characters, some of them known by name and others remaining anonymous (Marzolph 1998). *In this manner, the tales of the Arabic Juhâ, the Sicilian Giufà, the Sephardic Djoha, the Turkish Nasreddin Hoca, the Greek Nastratin, the Iranian Mollâ Nasreddin, the Özbek Ependi (Afandi) or the Chinese A-fan-ti derive from a common source.* Besides having been published in numerous jestbooks and cartoons, the tales attached to this character are alive in oral tradition and in a truly transnational manner are potentially accessible to virtually each and every inhabitant of the Muslim world. (Marzolph 2011, 182; emphases mine)

Unlike Djeha in this collection, who is more of an underdog or a parasite (see Déjeux 1976, 28 and 1978, 34), the Nasreddin Hoca character is usually portrayed as the village imam, a role that combines the functions of a judge (qadi), a teacher (hodja), and a preacher (imam); he is a figure who assists the community with legal and religious affairs (Başgöz and Boratav 1998, 7). The Turkish Nasreddin (also spelled Nasroddin) was originally a separate character that was only merged with Djeha/Juḥā/Ǧuḥā in a conscious effort in the nineteenth century during a period that also saw a speedy dissemination of a plethora of jocular folktale collections thanks to the introduction of the printing press in the Arab world (see Marzolph 1992, 1999, 2009, and 2011).[6]

The name of the North African Djeha/Juḥā/Ǧuḥā trickster has numerous dialectical variations throughout the
Mediterranean region, including Djeha, Djoha (Kabylia/
Algeria); Ch'ha, Ch'hâ, Djouha, Jeha, or Goha (Morocco,
Tunisia), Jeh'a, Jha, or Jh'a (Morocco); the Sicilian fool
called Giufà or Giucà; Jahan (Malta); Goha (Egypt); Joha
(Lebanon), and so on. The different spellings reflect the
hybridity and malleability of this transnational prankster
figure that has adapted to various cultural and geographical environments that boast ancestral oral storytelling
traditions.[7] As the Nasreddin character, the Juḥā character might also go back to a real person, though this cannot be proven: "First documented in third/ninth-century
Arabic literature, the character became especially popular
in Arabic and North African Berber tradition, but also in
Sephardic, Sicilian, Maltese, and mediaeval Persian traditions. Mediaeval historians and biographers tend to see
Juḥā as a person who lived in the second/eighth century"
(Marzolph 2017, 139–40). Trickster and jester stories started
circulating in Anatolia, Turkey, in the fifteenth century,
dating the existence of the character to the thirteenth or
fourteenth century.[8] According to Marzolph, the first documented Persian trickster collection contained 211 tales and
was published in 1299/1881, that is, forty-four years after the
first Turkish and seventeen years after the first Arabic print
edition (Marzolph 1991, 282). The name of the Ottoman
Turkish Nasroddin that preceded the Persian Nasreddin is
derived from Arabic: nasr al-adin means "victory of religion" (Leroy 1988, 8), and Hodja implies respect. Hodja is
a title reserved for the wise teacher, the one well-versed in
matters of Islamic practice and theology (Leeming 1979,
84). According to the "Naṣr al-Dīn Khodja" entry in the

online edition of the *Encyclopaedia of Islam*, "The first printed Turkish collection (Istanbul 1253/1837) comprises 134, later lithograph and printed collections some 125 anecdotes" (Marzolph, "Naṣr al-Dīn Khodja"). Today, two widely circulating books are the Egyptian collection *Akhbār Juḥā* (*The Anecdotes of Juha*) and the Kuwaiti collection *Juha al-ʿArabi* (*The Arabic Juha*; see Jayyusi 2007, 8).

Djeha and Jocular Literature in Islam

Historically, Islam does not go as far as encouraging humor, but it does legitimate it as a form of release and relaxation. The Prophet Muhammad is said to have had a cheerful disposition and a fairly good sense of humor (Marzolph 2000, 482). There are countless jokes and anecdotes in medieval Arabic literature.[9] Indeed, the history of early Muslim humor can be traced back to comedians from the Umayyad period (Rosenthal 1956, 5). Ashʿab the Greedy is a well-known prankster from the eighth century, but many other stock figures exist in medieval Arabic literature: the clever or dumb Bedouin, husbands and wives, and judges or members of other professions and crafts (Rosenthal 1956, 3). Popular Berber buffoons other than Djeha include Ben Cekran (the drunkard's son), Bou Naʾas (the sleeping man), Bou Kerch (the man with the belly), Bou Hamar (the donkey), and the prankster Si Mousa (Basset 1920, 179–80).

Today, Djeha remains beloved by generations of children and adults in the Maghreb (Algeria, Tunisia, Morocco, Mauritania), but also in Europe (Malta, Sicily, Ukraine, Armenia, Mongolia), the Middle East (Egypt, Iraq, Iran, Jordan, Lebanon, Pakistan, Afghanistan, Syria, Turkey,

Azerbaijan), Middle Asia (Turkestan, Turkmenistan, Uzbekistan), India, and Central Asia. The wise and foolish turban-clad trickster with his donkey is known everywhere in the Muslim world. He is popular because he embodies the revenge of the oppressed against the rich and powerful (Muzi 2009, 13). Often referred to as a wise fool or wise idiot, he recalls the buffoon or the king's jester at European courts or the court of Harûn al-Rashîd—the clever buffoon who pretends to be dumb and who makes everybody laugh at him. His enduring appeal can be attributed to the fact that he represents the humble and disenfranchised who dare to criticize corruption, dishonesty, greed, and abuse of power at any level of society (Galley and Iraqui Sinaceur 1994, 53).

The trickster is a universal character in mythology, folktales, and lore around the globe: African, Asian, Caribbean, European, Oceanic, Native American, and, of course, North African. The multifaceted popular Djeha figure appears in various genres (literature, movies, animation, comics, video games, plays, and popular culture artifacts) in many parts of the Muslim world. Well-known tricksters or comical characters or buffoons include Anansi (West Africa), the jester Till Eulenspiegel, the pranksters Max and Moritz (Germany), Don Quixote (Spain), Old Man Coyote (North America), the trickster Reynard the Fox (called Renart in France), Gargantua (France), and Gorakhnath (India), among many others. What exactly is a trickster? In their special issue of *Marvels and Tales* dedicated to trickster figures, the editors write:

> Subversive, deceptive, wily, and comical, the trickster spans national traditions, genres, and historical periods. Often represented as a deity, animal, or human,

between upper and lower worlds, the trickster functions as the creator and destroyer of worlds, embodies the sacred and the profane, and brings together
the scatological and the spiritual. In other tales, the
trickster is a lowly and seemingly unpromising hero
or a fool whose antics disrupt the social order only
temporarily. (Bacchilega and Duggan 2018, 10)

This definition aptly describes Djeha, who, we will see,
surely does not miss an opportunity to cause mayhem and
disruption. *The Greenwood Encyclopedia of Folktales and
Fairy Tales* defines the mythological trickster (as opposed
to the jester, or person using a ruse) as someone who

engages in trickery, deceives, and violates the moral
codes of the community. Oral and written tales associated with this pervasive figure are usually humorous, and the tales generally combine both comical
and satirical elements. The entertainment value of
trickster tales is predicated on not only the trickster's clever actions per se but also on the subversive
nature of his trickery. Members of his society derive
satisfaction from witnessing the sociopathic trickster violate social norms, often in fact to the benefit
of others, which can give him the status of a folk
hero. In this way, trickster tales also convey moral
lessons within a society. (Fernandes 2008, 992)

Though Djeha tales don't convey morals, since the
character usual displays immoral behavior, they are funny
and entertaining. Tricksters are usually male—as is the
case of Djeha—with the exception of the trickster-like

shrewd Shahrazad[10] from *The Arabian Nights*.[11] While
Djeha does not constantly live in the immediate threat
of being killed, he is a compulsive liar and uses his wits
to find sustenance. In that respect, he is a survivor, just
like the iconic Shahrazad. In most tales, he is poor and
hungry, often at the brink of starvation. As he laments to
his mother in the tale "Djeha and the Nail" (chapter 1), he
is forced to take desperate measures, such as selling his
house, in order to buy food and avoid starvation. When it
comes to finding food, he is clever, witty, and resourceful.
He relies on his intelligence, his creative problem-solving
skills, and his sense of humor to survive in an environment marked by a constant lack of food and material
resources. Djeha is poor but funny and creative. He will
do anything—even kill humans—to get food in his belly
(see chapter 6). He has a terrific sense of repartee that
makes for great stories or jokes. Occasionally, he kills animals (chickens, oxen, roosters, rabbits, sheep) and even
humans (the muezzin in "Djeha and the Sheep's Head,"
see chapter 6) to prove to his wife that he really is a sultan (king or sovereign of a Muslim state). Alternatively,
he incites other people to commit murder so that he
can keep the money that he conned out of them. In the
tale "Djeha's Knife Kills and Resuscitates" (chapter 6),
the thieves end up killing their own wives, because they
naïvely believe that Djeha owns a magical knife that lets
him administer punishment by killing and subsequently
bringing the dead back to life. He uses his naïve, inof-
fensively simple demeanor to cheat the gullible or trick
those who are stupid enough to trust his word. Though
he is a compulsive liar and a cheat, selfish and dishonest,
he is nevertheless a likable character, because he knows

how to crack a good joke at the right time and how to get people to laugh with him or, more often, laugh at him. As he declares in the tale "Djeha and the Miller" (chapter 3), "I am an idiot." And most people around him believe that he is indeed simpleminded or crazy.

The trickster is defined by his poverty, his liminality, and his violation of dominant norms. His behavior is transgressive and amoral. Though he is at the very bottom of the social order, he often manages to overthrow the hierarchical social order. At the beginning of the tale "Djeha Marries a Sultan's Daughter" (chapter 1), Djeha is essentially a beggar: destitute and clad in dirty rags. And yet he manages to marry the sultan's daughter, simply by performing a trick with dogs that makes her laugh for the first time in her life. Therefore, the sultan must honor his promise and give him the hand of his daughter. Djeha's nonconventional attitude disrupts the social order of society. He lies and occasionally breaks the law or threatens to disrupt the social order, as he does when he insults important dignitaries or ridicules the local qadi (Islamic judge). Djeha's proverbial laziness, his dishonesty, and his cunning attitude are subversive. He refuses to work for a living, and he occasionally murders people. Djeha is a social misfit, because he refuses to fully integrate himself into society, to be part of a system that "doesn't befit his taste for wandering aimlessly and leeching off of his acquaintances" (Bellagh 1987, 102–3). At a lecture given in 1957 at the École Pratique des Hautes Études, Tunisian philosopher and novelist Albert Memmi (1920–2020) remarked that the Djeha cycle is an "immensely collective narrative" that reveals how the man of the street sees himself and what ruses and stratagems he uses to survive (Déjeux 1978, 31 and 1995, 47).

In most of the tales, the trickster is old, destitute, and cunning, but in others he is young, naïve, vulnerable, and whimsical and gets told off by his mother. Though he appears to be generous at times, his generosity is never devoid of ulterior motives.[12] Djeha is highly intelligent, and he is quick witted and energetic when he needs to quickly find creative solutions to calm his hunger. Quite often, as in the tales "Djeha and the Treasure" (chapter 1), "Djeha and the Goat Hide" (chapter 1), and "Djeha in the Grave" (chapter 6), he teams up with his mother. The partners in crime use their wits to save their lives, find food or lodging, or con others (friends, robbers, strangers, monarchs, or animals) out of money or other objects that they can trade for food (see chapters 5 and 6). Generally, Djeha uses deception or ambiguous word play to trick his neighbors or friends (who usually turn out to be backstabbers) out of money, food, clothing, and other material things in order to ensure his survival and personal well-being (see chapter 4). In the tales "Djeha and the Thieves" and "The Hosts' Pickax" (chapter 5), Djeha tricks four thieves out of money by selling them a supposedly golden ass and a magical pickax that finds food in the ground.

North African Oral Tradition, Folktale Collectors, and Collections

Maghrebian trickster tales and folktales in general are part of a deeply ingrained, flourishing, and ancient oral tradition. Public storytelling and telling of folktales and anecdotes in North Africa started in the Middle Ages. In the eleventh century and thereafter, upper-class storytellers (called *rawi* or *fdawi*) told stories in public squares or in enclosed buildings such as mosques or cafés in front of a spellbound audience (Bouhdiba 1994, 7). Popular story-tellers or bards, such as the Algerian wandering poet Si Mohand (or M'hand) of the Aït Iraten tribe (born around 1840–1905 and dubbed the "Kabyle Verlaine"), were even paid to provide entertainment by putting on puppet shows. These performances provided welcome escapism. Tunisian sociologist and folklorist Abdelwahab Bouhdiba (1994, 9) divides Maghrebian folktales into four categories:

1. The *nadira*: a rare and strange anecdote such as the Djeha tales
2. The *hikaya*: a story that is based on real events
3. The *qissa*: a legendary myth that carries a symbolic or ontological dimension
4. The *kherrafa*: a folktale

According to Bouhdiba, the anecdotal character of the Djeha tales in Arabic is referred to as *nâdira* (also spelled *nadira*), an "outburst . . . witticism, sense of repartee, a vulgar or refined joke or an extraordinary or exceptional news story" (1994, 24). The narrative, tripartite structure of the trickster folktales is simple and can be summed up as follows:

1. The initial situation is described, which is nearly always a trivial everyday situation and is unrelated to situations recounted in other tales.
2. The trickster meets one or several characters that provoke or challenge him. This confrontation leads to a conflict or an imbalance of power. But

in some cases, the trickster turns out to be his own worst enemy.

3. Finally, the trickster's concluding quip, which is unexpected, shocking, or funny, wraps up the tale and leaves his challengers speechless and/or powerless. His concluding words signal the denouement and resolution of the initial conflict. These quips are funny and give the folktale its specific flavor (Maunoury 2011, 16). Unlike contemporary trickster variants that have been adapted into longer prose works (see Khiat 2016; Galley and Iraqui Sinaceur 1994; Delais 1986; Ben Danou 1971), many of Mouliéras's Djeha tales are short aphorisms.

It is only in the late nineteenth and early twentieth centuries that folktales, songs, and poems were finally recorded and written down for posterity, often by Catholic missionaries such as the Pères Blancs (White Fathers) but also by locals artists and writers.[13] Notable Francophone postcolonial folklore collectors of North African folktales include Nora Aceval (*Contes et traditions d'Algérie*, 2005; *Algerian Folktales and Traditions*), Rabah Belamri (*L'Oiseau du grenadier: contes d'Algérie*, 1985; *The Bird from the Pomegranate Tree: Algerian Folktales*), Christiane Achour (coedited with Zineb Ali-Benali: *Contes algériens*, 1989; *Algerian Folktales*), Salima Aït Mohamed (*Contes magiques de Haute Kabylie*, 1999; *Magic Folktales from Greater Kabylia*), Hocine Belhocine (*Contes du Djurdjura*, 2010; *Folktales from the Djurdjura*), Malika Halbaoui (*Contes des sages berbères*, 2016; *Folktales of the Wise Berbers*), Nacer Kemel (*Contes berbères*, 2014; *Berber Folktales*); Fatima Kerrouche (*Le Voyage de la reine Tin Hinan: contes berbères*, 2015 ; *Queen*

Tin Hinan's Journey: Berber Folktales), Mouloud Mammeri (*Machao!: contes berbères de Kabylie*, 1980; *Machao! Berber Tales from Kabylia*), Youssef Nacib (*Contes de Kabylie*, 1986; *Tales from Kabylia*), Larbi Rabdi (*Le Roi et les trois jeunes filles et autres contes berbères de Kabylie*, 2003; *The King and the Three Young Girls and Other Berber Tales from Kabylia*), Mélaz Yakouben (*Contes kabyles de Kabylie et de France*, 1997; *Berber Tales from Kabylia and France*), among others. While the preservation of ancestral oral folktales and traditions is at the forefront of all the collections by these collectors, editors and/or authors, it should be noted that even the most prolific collectors, in particular Nora Aceval and Rabah Belamri (1946–1995), are French Algerian citizens. All of these authors elect to write in French and publish their folktales in France with well-known publishing houses, such as Bordas, Flies France, Karthala, L'Harmattan, Publisud, or Seuil.[14] By choosing these Paris-based publishers, they ensure a wide dissemination of their books and gain access to a larger French-speaking readership. Most recently, Djeha has been reimagined by French Algerian folklorist Nora Aceval, whose feminist take on the trickster appeals to readers today. Aceval has transferred Djeha's ingenuity, cleverness, and wittiness to a female character—Djeha's clever wife—in her book *La Femme de Djha, plus rusée que le diable!* (2013; *Djha's Wife, More Cunning Than the Devil!*). This is only a logical step forward, given a plethora of Maghrebian tales and proverbs pointing out the intelligence and shrewdness of women (see Aceval 2005; Muzi 2003). Likewise, in Mouliéras's tales, the trickster's shrewd and conniving mother serves as a role model for Djeha.

French scholars and orientalists Auguste Mouliéras (1855–1931) and René Basset (1855–1924) were born into what had become a settler community (see Lorcin [1995] 2014, 10) and were among the first *pieds-noirs* (individuals of European descent born in Algeria before independence) to collect and translate popular Berber Djeha trickster tales into French. Though Mouliéras is credited with the publication of *Les Fourberies de Si Djeh'a*, it should be stressed that the book was in fact a collaborative effort between Auguste Mouliéras, folklorist René Basset, and Mouliéras's informants, who told Mouliéras the folktales that he wrote down and then translated into French. In the foreword to the 1892 edition of *Les Fourberies de Si Djeh'a*, Mouliéras thanks his friend and colleague René Basset for enriching his book with his comparative studies of the Djeha and Nasreddin Hoca characters in Turkish, Arab, and Berber source materials, and he further refers to his main informant as an "illiterate Kabyle of the Beni Jennad tribe" (1892, VII). In the preface of the first edition of *Légendes et contes merveilleux de la Grande Kabylie* (1893; *Legends and Marvellous Tales from Great Kabylia*), Mouliéras elaborates on the tale collection process and credits a man called Amor Ben Mohammed Ben Ali for recounting the Djeha tales to him:

> I collected the folktales published today three years ago from members of the Beni Jennad El-Bahar tribe, who worked as masseurs at the Turkish Bath of the Grande Mosquée, also known as the Mosquée de Pacha. *Among them, I must specially mention Amor Ben Mohammed Ben Ali to whom I owe Les Fourberies de Si Djeh'a.* One of his claims was to pretend that he held the monopoly of folktales and popular legends in his tribe, thus silencing, perhaps

intentionally, the traditions that still exist among the Zwawa tribe today; for they have, in fact, up to the present delivered the richest harvest, among the Berbers of northern Algeria. However, it was not difficult to see that the issue of invention got lost in the mist of time: at the most, he suspected that some of these tales might have been borrowed from the Arabs. (1893, I; emphasis mine)

Born in Tlemcen[15] in 1833, shortly after the beginning of the French colonization of Algeria (1830–1962), Auguste Mouliéras wore many hats: he was a translator for the French government, an anthropologist, a grammarian, a missionary, and a professor of Arabic studies in Oran. From 1872 to 1893, he crisscrossed Morocco and published a two-volume book about his travels in 1895–1899, titled *Le Maroc inconnu: 22 ans d'explorations dans cette contrée mystérieuse, de 1872 à 1893* (*The Unknown Morocco: Twenty-Two Years of Explorations in This Mysterious Area from 1872 to 1893*). Mouliéras was foremost an academic and teacher of Arabic and by no means a trained ethnographer (see Burke 2014, 147–49 about his ill-fated trip to Fez). Given his linguistic expertise and native proficiency in both French and Arabic, he was a talented translator and, fortunately for us, a prolific disseminator of, as American historian Edmund Burke writes, "irrelevant folklore" (2014, 21).[16] An accomplished scholar and folklorist, Mouliéras also traveled in his native Algeria and notably in Kabylia, the mountainous region in northern Algeria known for its ancestral oral tradition. In Kabylia, he collected hundreds of oral Berber tales that he wrote down, translated into French, and published in his monumental collection

Légendes et contes merveilleux de la Grande Kabylie (1823; *Legends and Marvelous Tales from Great Kabylia*), which was later reedited by French ethnologist and folklorist Camille Lacoste-Dujardin in a collection titled *Traduction des légendes et contes de la Grande Kabylie recueillis par Auguste Mouliéras* (1965; *Translation of Legends and Tales from Great Kabylia collected by Auguste Mouliéras*).

French orientalist and missionary René Marie Joseph Basset (born in Lunéville, Meurthe-et-Moselle, France in 1855 and died in Algiers in 1924) was a professor of Arabic and a dean at the University of Algiers. He was the first director of the École des lettres d'Alger, created in 1879. A Berber specialist, folklorist, historian, and linguist, René Basset was a prolific scholar who published over one hundred books in his lifetime, including several folktale collections: *Contes arabes: histoires des dix vizirs* (1883; *Arab Folktales: Stories of the Ten Viziers*), *Contes populaires berbères* (1887; *Popular Berber Tales*), *Mille et un contes, récits et légendes arabes* (1924–1926; *One Thousand and One Tales, Stories and Arab Legends*), *Nouveaux contes berbères* (1897; New Berber Tales), and *Contes populaires d'Afrique* (1903; *Popular African Tales*). Mouliéras's *Les Fourberies de Si Djeh'a* features the sixty folktales followed by "A Study of Djeha and Anecdotes Attributed to Him" ("Étude sur Djeh'a et les anecdotes qui lui sont attribuées"), an appendix authored by René Basset. Though they were researchers at heart, it cannot be denied that August Mouliéras, René Basset, and his son (historian and linguist Henri Basset) were orientalist scholars and part of a colonial ethnographic system that was imbued with prejudice and racist stereotypes under France's Third Republic (1870–1940). Colonial diplomats, ethnographers, administrators, and even generals (see Hanoteau 1867; Hanoteau and Letourneux 1872–1873) produced an impressive body of texts about Islam that informed French imperial politicians, officials, and diplomats about local customs and traditions as well as the "mentality" of the Berber people. These publications led to the construction of the well-known Kabyle myth, according to which the sedentary Berbers were superior to Arabs. As historian Patricia Lorcin wrote in her seminal study *Imperial Identities: Stereotyping, Prejudice, and Race in Colonial Algeria* (first published in 1995 and again in 2014), the Kabyle myth can be seen in a "body of work extolling the Kabyles and denigrating the Arabs" (Lorcin [1995] 2014, 11). When reading and interpreting these trickster tales in the twenty-first century, caution is warranted. It must be kept in mind that Mouliéras was an educated white male and enjoyed what today would be referred to as white privilege. He was a university professor in a settler colony, and he might have been somewhat prejudiced against the local population. Born and raised in French Algeria, he was foremost a professor and a highly prolific and passionate scholar and researcher. However, he was a cog in a wider colonial project and, therefore, the cultural, political, and ideological undertones of these folktales cannot be ignored. From a contemporary point of view, Mouliéras can, thus, be accused of implicit bias when transcribing these tales, simply because he was himself part of a powerful colonial empire in a settler colony where the Muslim population was denied full citizenship rights (unlike the Jewish population in Algeria, which had become naturalized French through the Crémieux Laws in 1870). Frictions between various religious factions are apparent in chapter 6 ("Religion, Death, and the Afterlife"), where it is difficult to determine whether or not some racists stereotypes linked to Judaism and Islam—but also, it should be highlighted, Christianity (see "Djeha and the Christian" in chapter 6)—reflect Mouliéras's own beliefs. That said, the fact that identical variants of tales featuring Muslim, Jewish, and Christian stock characters can be found in Egyptian (see Finbert 1929) and in Sephardic Jewish collections (see Koén-Sarano 2003) indicates that certain stereotypes linked to Judaism, Christianity, and Islam do not reflect Mouliéras's personal opinions but were deeply ingrained stereotypes in these societies at that time.

Finally, German explorer and ethnologist Leo Viktor Frobenius (1873–1938) also revisits the prankster in his folklore collection *Volksmärchen der Kabylen* (1921–1922).[17] Frobenius highlights the breadth and variety of storytelling performances and the dazzling number of Djeha variants in circulation. Frobenius writes, "Dscheha or Djeha is one of the most famous characters in Kabyle storytelling. People tell each other various pranks that follow one another in varying order. The endings also vary greatly from one version (variant) to another" (1921–1922, 187; my translation). In the twentieth century, French Christian missionary Jean Déjeux (1921–1993), a religious scholar (Père Blanc, or White Father) and an eminent scholar on Maghreb literature, reedited Mouliéras's 1892 Djeha edition. His book, *Les Fourberies de Si Djeh'a: contes kabyles* (published in 1987), is a bilingual (Berber-French) reedition of Mouliéras's tales. Déjeux also revisited the trickster in *Djoh'a: héros de la tradition orale arabo-berbère: hier et aujourd'hui* (1978), and in two scholarly articles (see Déjeux 1976, 1995).

Who Is Djeha and Why Did He Become a Trickster?

In Mouliéras's collection, little emerges about Djeha's background or identity. In the tale "Djeha and the Treasure" (chapter 1), the storyteller laconically explains, "When Djeha was a child, he was a bit innocent and ignorant: when he grew up a bit, he became smarter." However, there is a German variant, simply titled "Djeha," that provides a plausible explanation of why he becomes a liar, a cheat, and a trickster in the first place. According to this tale, he was at first an honest, industrious, hardworking farmer, diligently plowing his field with his two oxen, heeding his mother's advice to be good, and desperately trying to make an honest living. Yet, after a while, he came to the realization that all his efforts were fruitless, because he was still dirt poor. After making the mistake of entrusting his two oxen to two strangers to watch and having both his oxen and his only livelihood stolen, Djeha swore revenge and changed. From this day onward, he used his intelligence to outwit everybody and to trick and manipulate people in order to have a better life and to avoid starvation (see Frobenius 1921–1922, 187–89).

In Mouliéras's folktale collection, descriptions of the trickster's physical appearance are quasiabsent and the sixty tales do not form a coherent entity. In most tales, he is either a farmer, a peasant, a merchant, a butcher, or unemployed. In the tale "Djeha and His Donkey" (chapter 2), we learn that he deserves respect, because he is old and has a white beard. In other tales, he is a numbskull or portrayed as young, inexperienced, innocent, or naïve. People take advantage of him because his father is no longer alive to protect and guide him. This is because, over the centuries, the repertoire of Djeha tales increased and the depiction of the character itself changed.[18] The innocent and charming version of the character appears in the tale "Djeha and the Thieves" (chapter 5), for example, where he trades his mule for a donkey and purchases a broken dish. His mother accuses him of being naïve and gullible. Geographical or temporal clues are sparse in these tales. In "The High-Strung Horse" (chapter 2), Djeha is given the mission to deliver a letter to the bey of Algiers, but the leader is not named. In the tale "The Rent" (chapter 2), mention is made of the Aïssaouas, a religious and mystical brotherhood founded in Meknes, Morocco, by Sheikh al-Kamil Mohamed al-Hadi ben Issa (or Aissa; 1465–1526). The members of the Aïssaouas were known for their rituals that involved dancing, animal sacrifices, and the ingestion of animals such scorpions, toads, and snakes accompanied by women's ululation. Such specific references to the Maghreb are rare.

Is Djeha a Saint or a Madman?

If saints' lives are marked by generosity, sacrifice, and self-lessness (Dermenghem 1954, 329), then the trickster surely is the opposite of a saint. However, given the overlapping of the concepts of saints and madness in the Maghreb, the wise trickster possesses certain qualities that link him to the idea of madness. This is because in the Maghreb, the concepts of marginality, madness, and potentially subversive difference incarnated by Djeha oscillate greatly. In Persia, for instance, the trickster is referred to as a wise figure of religious authority, a mullah (educated Muslim trained in religious law and doctrine and usually holding an official post). In other tales, he often appears to be a buffoon or the village idiot.[19] In this collection, the trickster is disrespectful of important religious rituals, in particular the calls to prayer. He is a dangerous criminal who murders a muezzin so that his mother may sleep through the night without being awakened by the calls to prayers ("Djeha and the Sheep's Head," chapter 6). Unlike in Western society, where in the nineteen and twentieth centuries the development of medicine and the concept of mental illness led to the internment of the mentally ill in mental institutions (see Foucault 1965), in the Maghreb, madmen were tolerated and roamed the streets freely: "Every North African village has its 'madman' wandering the streets cursing or laughing out loud. Each village has its 'Bouchta,' its Moha or Z'id Ahmed. These madmen, who one is afraid to look at because they like to display their intimacy and have a shocking demeanor, are most often commonplace cases in Arab-Muslim society" (Bekkay 1984, 4). However, unlike in the West, the various figures that embody these unconventional qualities or potentially dangerous character traits are not marginalized but celebrated as mystical[20] or religious figures, bearers of truth, or as individuals endowed with magical powers, such as the baraka. Sorcery and magic flourished in medieval North Africa (see Dols 1992, 281) and are still important today (see, e.g., Taïa 2000). In the context of ancestral Berber/Amazigh and Kabyle mythology, the madman, *iassasn*,[21] was considered an incarnation of a protective spirit who guarded people and their homes. Further types of madmen include the post-Islamic *majdoub* (mystics who have access to divination) in Sufism and the *majnoun*, individuals possessed by djinns (spirit, supernatural power) who, in pre-Islamic times, received messages from genies, which they then proclaimed like oracles in rhymed prose (Diop 2005, 257–58). Twenty-first-century Western readers will be astounded by the complexity of the various overlapping or merging concepts of saintliness and madness. Madmen and saints in Islam include fools called *bahlul*, or *mahboul* (crazy person, village idiot) and alienated madmen called *mejnoun* (Dermenghem 1954, 29). The so-called *mejdoub* (saint/madman) belongs to a specific category of saints who have had their spirits ravished and risk staying *mejdoub* all their lives: they are "authentic mystics with uncontrollable impulses as well as dim-witted individuals" (Dermenghem 1954, 21). As the late medieval social historian Michael Walter Dols states, the wise fool *buhloul* is "the only humorous character in Islamic literature that has survived to the present day from the Middle Ages aside from Nasreddin Hodja, the comparable figure in Turkish literature.... He represents the clever, seemingly mad critic of society and its values" (1992, 356).[22] Such mad individuals—like Djeha in this collection—enjoy roaming the streets, or sometimes they keep to themselves: "They survive thanks to charity, which they never lack. They follow their impulses. They paradoxically express profound truths" (Dermenghem 1954, 29). They are social outcasts that lead nomadic lifestyles and have rare insights. They share some commonalities with the sort of marginalized, poor figure incarnated by Djeha in this collection, given his clairvoyance, his at times sarcastic humor, and his criticism of social inequalities.

Charity—the third pillar of Islam—emerges as an important aspect of the tales: "Muhammad's primary concern was for individual salvation: paradise is specifically promised to those who are charitable. The focus is clearly on the spiritual benefit to the giver rather than on the material benefit to the recipient; the poor did the almsgiver a necessary service" (Dols 1992, 460). Charity and almsgiving as stipulated by the Qur'an appear in the tales "Djeha and the Rabbit Sauce" (chapter 2) and "The Turnips" (chapter 4), where Djeha is given a gift. In Islam, there are two types of charity: *sadaqa*, meaning alms of spontaneity or private alms, and *zakāt*, obligatory alms taxes (see Dols 1992, 460). The gift giving in these tales is of a private freewill nature. As medieval historian Michael W. Dols writes, "The basic intent of charity was not primarily the eradication of the causes of distress, as in the modern notion of philanthropy but the alleviation of its effects. Within this general context, the insane were of importance to the state primarily as a potential threat to internal peace and harmony" (1992, 462).

Djeha, a Universal Character Who Looms Large in Children's Literature

The trickster's conflicting character traits reflect universal truths about the inherent ambivalence of human nature— wisdom and idiocy, circumspection and foolishness, generosity and greediness. Djeha is a Janus-faced, ambivalent character. He is likable yet egotistical and/or dangerous, sometimes a harmless jokester, or prankster, sometimes a murderer.[23] With all his flaws and foibles, Djeha is a profoundly human and universal character whose unpredictable conduct mirrors human interaction across time and nations. In the twentieth century, Djeha tales spread to North America thanks to the Californian diaspora (see

Byrnum 1989). Even today, Djeha invites us to think about who we are as individuals in our respective communities and why we act the way we do and say the things we say in a given situation or social interaction. In that respect, these tales remain relevant, because Djeha functions as a folktale antihero who purports to serve as a role model.[24] In the tale "Djeha and His Wife" (chapter 1), Djeha pretends to act as a role model, but in reality he blatantly transgresses sacred and secular rituals associated with holidays, a popular folklore genre (see Sims and Stephens, 2005). He tells his wife that even though he doesn't need the money, he has to go to work on a religious holiday, so that the common people follow his example and avoid starving. The trickster's shadow looms large in children's literature, where he fulfills a pedagogical function by teaching ancestral traditions and rites of passage.

The character is even used to teach Arabic (see Al-Hakkak, 2018). In many of these children's and young adult books, the trickster character functions as an intergenerational link between children born in France and parents and/or grandparents born in North Africa (or elsewhere in the Middle East where the trickster figure is ubiquitous). This is because the nature of storytelling itself has fundamentally changed over the past century. Traditionally, storytellers in North Africa were mostly older women. The folktales and legends were handed down by grandmothers by the fireplace, or *kanoun* (portable oven made of clay), to their grandchildren (see Aïtel 2014, 172). Today, of course, modern amenities, satellite dishes, and the internet are present even in the most remote mountain areas. The rural population is far more likely to watch American or French television or Egyptian soap operas than to listen to oral folktales. Furthermore, the gradual erosion of the traditional patriarchal family structure has accelerated the disintegration of traditionally larger, intergenerational family clans. Many young couples, for instance, move to urban areas or settle down in villages by themselves, creating smaller nuclear families. It is becoming increasingly rare to have three generations under the same roof, which is necessary to facilitate the transmission of oral folktales (Nacib 1982, 1–2). Hence, literary juvenile folktales, though they are not a substitute for ancestral oral story-telling traditions, at least allows for the preservation and perpetuation of an oral heritage. Lastly, the internet also plays a major role in disseminating traditional folktales.

The tales in juvenile collections focus on the trickster's wittiness and recount his struggle for survival in an eco-nomically harsh environment. Generally, Djeha tales for children insist on the trickster's cleverness, his sense of repartee, his ingenuity and resourcefulness (see Khiat 2016), or his combined wisdom and madness (see Zouaoui 2017). The juvenile collections feature the most popular tales: "Djeha's Nail," "Goha Counts His Donkeys" (Djeha is unsure whether he owns eleven or twelve donkeys, depend-ing on whether or not he counts the donkey he is riding), "Goha Decides to Buy a New Donkey," and "Goha Tricks the Robbers."[25] All of the Algerian, French, and binational editors of these children's folktale collections highlight the importance of passing down an important cultural folktale heritage, as French novelist and journalist Jean Coué writes in *Djeha le malin* (1993; *Djeha, the Shrewd One*): "How can you tell that Kabylia is one of the most beautiful areas of Algeria? It is the most beautiful. And, by the way, it is the birthplace of Djeha!" (9).

Chapter 1

Family and Kinship

In traditional North African Berber tribes such as the one depicted in these folktales, authority is wielded by the father and the extended paternal branch of the family (i.e., the father's brothers and sisters), whereas the mother and maternal branch are said to be softer, more forgiving, and more emotional (Galley and Iraqui Sinaceur 1994, 51). Interestingly, the present collection is marked by a nontraditional family structure and a paternal power vacuum. There is no mention of whether the trickster has any brothers and sisters. In fact, he appears to be an only child. Likewise, Djeha's father is only mentioned in six tales, one of which recounts his burial ("The Burial of Djeha's Father" in chapter 1). Djeha decides to bury his father in a very public place—the souk (market)—as if he wanted to ascertain that everyone knows that, though orphaned, he had a father and that the patriarch has passed his authority on to him and secured him a permanent place in the market. Djeha's disregard for religious beliefs and violation of common funeral practices with regard to his father's unorthodox burial mirrors practices linked to vernacular religion in other tales (see chapter 6). The transfer of power and authority is symbolized by

the farcical pars pro toto figure of one of his father's feet
sticking out of the ground. Djeha uses his father's foot as
a stake that he drives into the ground and to which he ties
his donkey to permanently reserve his vendor spot at the
market. In other collections (such as those of the Moroccan
Colin archives, the so-called Fond Colin), the trickster has
no father or if he does, he is never mentioned (see Galley
and Iraqui Sinaceur 1994). The quasiabsence of the father/
patriarch is undoubtedly necessary for the prankster to
assert himself as the strong, freewheeling folk antihero that
he is. The Berber Djeha epitomizes the *Imazighen*—free
people—as the Berbers refer to themselves. The folk protagonist's family as it is depicted in this folktale collection
reflects the tendency in traditional Berber families of being
"almost always monogamous" (Basset 1920, 144).[1] But again,
the family structure is atypical in that it does not constitute
an extended family. The traditional Berber family structure
"brings together all the agnates (descendants from a common male ancestor), thereby uniting several generations
in intimate association and communion under a single
chief" (Bourdieu 1961, 3). Obviously, given the aphoristic
or anecdotal form of most of the folktales, such large family structures would be impossible to accommodate in the
narrative genre of the popular folktale. More importantly, it
would draw attention away from the prankster protagonist,
his feats and misdeeds.

Historically, the family structure in Kabylia was strictly
patriarchal (see Bourdieu 1961, chapter "The Kabyles"). The
agnate patriarchal family structure and socioeconomic cohe-
sion of tribes was ensured by arranging marriages between
cousins, namely sons with the daughters of paternal uncles
(Cherif [1995] 2004a, 100). Today, this practice is no longer

necessarily applied in all domains or geographical areas. For instance, many young Kabyle women, notably college graduates, choose their own husbands by suggesting to their parents whom they want to marry, something that "would have been inconceivable before the war of independence" (Nacib 2002, 61), the war that lasted from 1954 to 1962 and led to independence from France. Postindependence, traditional patriarchal family structures continue to change due to the decline of agricultural activity, a rural exodus, and emigration, among other factors (see Lacoste-Dujardin [1995] 2004). Nonetheless, gender inequalities in the Maghreb subsist in Algeria in particular (and to a lesser extent in Tunisia and Morocco, where women enjoy considerably more civil rights). The birth of a child is welcomed in the Maghreb, particularly if the baby is a boy (Nacib 1981, 9). Algerian folklorist Youssef Nacib (1981, 10) notes that women sing songs on this special occasion:

A tender boy was born
It is the Creator who gave it
Glory to Him

Traditionally, the birth of a baby girl has often been greeted by family members with much less enthusiasm (see Lacoste-Dujardin 1987). While sons guarantee the continuation of the male lineage and family clan, daughters are seen as potential threats to the family's honor if they were to lose their virginity before getting married. As French philosopher and sociologist Pierre Bourdieu remarks, the power of patriarchy was strong in traditional Kabyle society, even in the mid-twentieth century, when he was writing these lines:

Marriage liberates a woman from the absolute authority of her father only to hand her over to the complete domination of her husband, or, more precisely, to the domination of her husband's family group and particularly of her mother-in-law. She must be both an obedient and faithful wife. With marriage, her former fear of losing her virginity is replaced by the fear of sterility, which she seeks to ward off by amulets, pilgrimages, votive offerings and all sorts of magical rites. The husband has complete liberty to end the marriage. He merely has to pronounce the formula of repudiation in the presence of friends, of a marabout [healer; living descendants of saintly lineages possessing magical powers (baraka)] of the assembly or, at the present time, before the cadi (or qadi, a minor judge or magistrate). (Bourdieu 1961, 6–7)

In reality, gender relations were (and remain) much more nuanced and complex than strictly patriarchal. A Kabyle proverb portrays Berber women as outspoken and much less oppressed and submissive than Bourdieu's observations would suggest. Women often ruled their households; they were the decision makers in their homes, as a well-known proverb states: "The house is his, the decision is hers" (Nacib 2002, 62). The female characters in these folktales, Djeha's mother and wife, are stubborn and clever (his mother), or rich and demanding (his wife). Still, in the tale "Djeha and His Wife," the trickster does not listen to his wife's injunction not to work, thus breaking a religious law that forbids work on religious holidays, such as Ashura,[2] or Aïd Al Adha[3] (see Haddadou 2000, 141). Interestingly,

Djeha does not have a daughter in this folktale collection, but he does have a son, who is mentioned only once, in the tale "Djeha and His Son." There is no mention of an extended family. Instead, readers are presented with a small nuclear family[4] made up mostly of the trickster, his mother, or his wife. Traditionally, in Berber society, space was divided along gender lines. In these tales however, the dichotomy of space—women/inside (house, garden, childrearing, cooking/food and the secret world of intimate life, sexuality) versus men/outside (public life marked by social and political activities and exchanges, assembly, mosque, fields, markets)[5]—is not always strictly observed. In Berber villages, women could walk freely from house to house, to fountains (called *tala*) or wells (called *ibir*) to fetch water, and to the fields (Nacib 1981, 98). Their responsibilities included taking care of children and all of the household chores (milling; churning butter; cooking; cleaning; sewing; weaving carpets, blankets, and burnouses; and laundry; see "Djeha and His Burnous" in this chapter). Women also sorted grains and fetched water from the village fountain. They were expected to do gardening, help out with harvests, and work in the fields (as in the tale "Djeha, the Field, and the Old Woman" in chapter 3). Given the traditional Kabyle division of labor—men plowing the fields and women staying mostly indoors weaving and taking care of the household and children—it seems unusual for Djeha's wife to ask him to watch their son in the tale "Djeha and His Son." The trickster's childish reaction—he urinates on his son— constitutes a gross violation of Muslim rituals related to the precept of purity in Islam: "The shariat[6] includes thousands of rules that define polluting and purifying actions for the believers. Blood, semen, urine, dogs, non-Muslims,

and many other things are deemed najes, ritually unclean"
(Afary and Afary 2018, 26–27). Djeha also urinates on a
man in the tale "Djeha and the Qadi" (chapter 3), again
violating socioreligious norms. The ambivalent trickster
character combines incompatible dimensions, in particular
the spiritual (frequent invocations of God that allow Djeha
to cement his authority and gain credibility in the village
community) and the scatological or the bawdy: allusions
to bodily functions, sexuality, and alcohol consumption
(see "Djeha and His Son," "Djeha and the Local Caid," and
"Djeha and the Qadi"). In the tale "Djeha and His Wife,"
the trickster's outrageous behavior serves to remind his
wife of his patriarchal privileges. He basically tells her that
it is her job, not his, to take care of their child. The tale
reflects traditional gender divisions regarding child care, as
Berber scholar Mohand Akli Haddadou highlights: Berber
women from Kabylia had to obey their husbands but were
allowed to leave the home to work in the fields (2000,
192). By contrast, the trickster's place is outside, not in the
home, because he is a man. However, Djeha is a transgressive character, because he refuses to work, an attitude that
makes him a social outcast, a folktale antihero. The trickster occasionally bends the law or subverts the hierarchical
social order, as he does in the tale "Djeha Marries a Sultan's
Daughter." Transgression is not necessarily associated with
murder or crime. Often Djeha violates social norms and
expectations simply by being idle and refusing to be a pro-
ductive member of the village community:

> Work is neither an end in itself nor a virtue per se.
> What is valued is not action directed towards an
> economic goal, but activity in itself, regardless of its

economic function and merely on condition that it has a social function. The self-respecting man must always be busy doing something. . . . A lazy person is not fulfilling the function incumbent on him as a member of the group: he thereby sets himself on the edge of society and runs the risk of being cast out. (Bourdieu 1979, 24)

Kabyle men were expected to work outside of the home, barter, socialize, and engage with other men. They had to be careful to avoid unwanted or undesirable encounters:

A self-respecting man must leave the house at daybreak; morning is the day of the daytime and leaving the house in the morning is a birth. Hence the importance of the things encountered, which are important for the whole day, so that in the event of an undesirable encounter (a smith, a woman carrying an empty leather bag, shouts, or a quarrel, a deformed being), it is better to go back and "remake one's morning" or one's "going out." (Bourdieu 1979, 149)

Unfortunately, Djeha has many unwanted encounters (see the robber tales in chapter 5) and often asks his mother (and sometimes his wife) for advice on how to get out of trouble. The traditional dichotomy of space applies to many tales, as it is generally the trickster (and not his mother or wife) who regularly goes to the market to buy, sell, or trade oxen, donkeys, goats, beef, pots, or casserole dishes. The Algerian folktale "Why Women Were Not Allowed to Go to the Market" ("Pourquoi le souk fut interdit aux femmes") sheds light on why women were not allowed to go to the market: "A long time ago, women went to the market where they spent their time gossiping instead of making a profit. They also neglected their homes and their children. This is why their husbands no longer allowed them to go there anymore" (Aceval 2005, 29–30).

In keeping with a well-known Mediterranean proverb, "Only the Creator can subdue women" (Galley and Iraqui Sinaceur 1994, 55), women are reputed to be clever, manipulative, and shrewd. Female shrewdness[7] is symbolized by Djeha's highly intelligent mother. The tale "Djeha and the Goat Hide" in this chapter illustrates the close relationship between the trickster and his shrewd widowed mother, his closest ally and partner in crime. She is a role model for Djeha, as is his father, who in the tale "Djeha and the Murder Victim" instructs him on what to do in order to avoid getting accused of murder when a man's corpse is found in Djeha's house (see chapter 6). But most often, it is his mother whom the trickster asks for advice. He often praises her problem-solving skills, as in the tale "Djeha and the Pot," where he informs the buyer of the pot that his mother always filled the hole in the pot with cotton balls to keep it from leaking. In the tale "Djeha and the Treasure," his mother saves the day and successfully masks the trickster's lack of discretion (he naïvely tells everybody that he is rich because he found a treasure) by making it rain crêpes and eggs so that the villagers won't believe him when he claims that he found and brought home a treasure.[8] Evidently, Djeha in this tale is still young and naïve and wants to be a good son. He does not want to be seen treasure hunting, and he also does not want to be seen stealing a treasure that he thinks belongs to an owl. Treasure hunting as an activity might strike the contemporary reader as odd, but this has not always been the case. In his magisterial study *The Muqaddimah*, Maghrebian historian Ibn Khaldun (1332–1406), the "founder of sociology or even political economy and surely one of the most important historians of all times" (Lacoste [1995] 2004, 15) morally condemns this apparently widespread habit. Treasure hunting, Ibn Khaldun argued, is for weak-minded people who refuse to work for a living: "Trying to make money from buried and other treasures is not a natural way of making a living" (Rosenthal 1969, 301). According to Ibn Khaldun, treasure hunting is a waste of time and no one should be systematically searching for a treasure (Rosenthal 1969, 303). This perception is consistent with teachings of the Qur'an, which considers a preoccupation with worldly riches to be "a hindrance to true piety" (Dols 1992, 460). Books on treasures and treasure hunting constitute a specific genre in Arabic literature. Treasures hold an important place in the North African and Middle Eastern imaginary, as illustrated in the many folktales that mention them. In the tale "Ali Baba and the Forty Thieves," a tale by the Syrian narrator Hanna Diyab that is commonly acknowledged as part of *The Arabian Nights*, Ali Baba and his clever servant Morgiane go to great lengths to keep their discovery of a treasure and the subsequent murder of the thieves a secret from the village community. They believe the villagers would envy them for their unexpected fortune, possibly kill them, and steal their treasure. In "Sinbad the Sailor," Sindbad, a seafaring merchant, brings back treasures from each of his seven journeys and retires in exceptional wealth and luxury. In North Africa, legend has it that when the Romans and Christians (whose kings and queens were immensely wealthy) left the country precipitously after the Muslim conquest, they were unable to take their treasures with them. They buried them in the ground or left them in the caves they had inhabited. To keep the population from stealing their treasures, they ordered genies to guard them from any pillagers (Basset 1920, 247). In his intellectual biography of Ibn Khaldun, Islamicist Robert Irwin states that Ibn Khaldun linked treasure hunting to the equally bad practices of alchemy and sorcery:

> Alchemy tended to be taken up by people who were too lazy to do a proper day's work. *Similarly, forgers and treasure hunters should have their hands cut off.* Since treasures were widely believed to be protected by spells and curses, the pseudoscience of treasure hunting had occult resonances. Those brave and gullible enough to follow the professional treasure hunter had to steel themselves to face ancient curses, monsters, death-dealing automata, and lethal trap-doors. Confidence tricksters used bogus maps and they might salt the alleged site of some great treasure with small quantities of gold and silver. In this way, they secured funding for their spurious expeditions from gullible patrons. *Underlying feverish quest for hidden treasures was the sense that both the Maghreb and Egypt had been much wealthier in Pharaonic and Roman times. Where had all the gold and jewels gone?* Ibn Khaldun very sensibly suggested much of the past wealth of the Maghreb and Egypt had passed on to other regions such as India and Europe, while other treasures had been melted down or crumbled to dust. (2018, 124; emphases mine)

The multiple references to a treasure in the midst of ruins in the tale "Djeha and the Treasure" (this chapter) seems to mirror the character's longing for a more glorious, richer past. Unfortunately, poverty is the trickster's lot in life. In the widely disseminated tale "Djeha and the Nail," the trickster tells his (at first) skeptical mother that he sold their house (except for a nail in the wall), so that they may buy food with the money. In another variant ("Djeha's Nail"), the trickster sells his house (except for the prover-bial nail) to a rich and greedy neighbor, who also ends up giving it back to him because he grows tired of Djeha visiting his home every day to stare at his beloved nail. In colloquial Arabic parlance, the word *masmar* means both "nail" and "greedy" in a figurative sense (Khiat 2016, 19). In both Tunisia and Algeria, this tale is so well known that the proverb "Remember Ch'hâ's Nail" is commonly used to warn someone against a tricky clause in a contract (see Nahum 1998, 12; Déjeux 1978, 29 and 1987, 18).[9] Indeed, in an Algerian variant of the tale, titled "Le Clou de Djoha" ("Djoha's Nail"), the trickster hires a judge and dictates a sales contract with one clause granting him exclusive ownership of the nail (Ben Danou 1971, 61–63). "Beware of Djoha's Nail" is a popular proverb used to warn someone against incurring unnecessary risks (Ben Danou 1971, 63).

In the tale "Djeha and His Burnous," which again uses a pars pro toto motif for dramatic effect, the trickster lei-surely watches his wife, who is busy washing their clothes in the river. She hangs up his burnous to dry. Hanging from a tree, the burnous looks like a man, so much so that a man takes a shot at it. He is convinced that he just killed Djeha. However, the trickster bursts out laughing, because he successfully tricked his adversary into believing that he's dead. His wife is shocked, considering that Djeha does not own a lot of clothes and, more importantly, given the symbolism[10] linked to the burnous, which endows its wearer with masculine honor (Lacoste-Dujardin 2003, 68). The burnous is not just any ordinary piece of clothing. It is an extension of the man itself. According to Algerian folklorist Youssef Nacib, its function is to "protect from the cold and to affirm a man's personality; the burnous is majestic, warm and resistant at once" (1981, 33).

Djeha and His Son

One day, Djeha's wife handed him their three-month-old son and said: "Look after your son, I have chores to do. Watch him for me until I have finished my work."

As Djeha was holding the baby on his lap, his son peed on him. Djeha put the baby on the ground and reciprocated. Alarmed by what she witnessed, his wife came running.

"What on earth are you doing, Djeha?"

"This little rascal urinated on me, so I also urinated back at him. If someone other than my son had done this, I would have defecated on him."

Djeha and the Pot

One day, he went to the market to sell his pot.

"That pot is full of holes. It's going to leak. It's completely useless," people said to him.

Djeha said, "This pot doesn't leak. My mother always filled it with cotton balls and not a single one leaked out."

Djeha and the Nail[11]

The very day he put his house up for sale, a man agreed to buy it.

"My friend," Djeha said to him, "I sold the house to you. However, remember that I did not sell you that nail in the wall over there. Now, tomorrow, don't go about saying, 'You also sold me the nail.' I didn't sell it to you; I only sold the house to you."

"That's fine, I'm buying the house. I'm not buying that nail in the wall."

The buyer thought to himself, "I don't care about the nail. I bought the house. Why care about a nail?"

Djeha went looking for his mother.

"Oh Mother, how many days have we spent hungry? Today, I sold our house."

"Djeha, are you out of your mind? You sold the house! And where will we live? Not only are we starving, but we will also have to sleep under the stars?"

"Dear Mother, don't worry. I sold the house to him. But I still own a nail that I hammered into the wall. I didn't sell him that nail. Now, it is with this nail that I will take the house back from him. We are starving to death. I came up with this ruse so that the buyer would give us money, so that we can buy food. Trust me, he will move out of the house."

"Seriously? You sold the house to him and you're saying that *he* will move out of it? Do you really believe that he will vacate the premises? He handed you the money in front of witnesses!"

"You just wait and take it easy. I will use my brains to work out a plan to make him move out of the house."

"Do as you wish."

Djeha left to buy animal skins and hung them from the nail. He also left entrails dangling from the nail. He left the pelts and entrails hanging there, and one or two days later, they started to stink. Djeha left them hanging there. The new house owner came looking for him.

"What kind of a deal is this, Djeha? You came and left skins and entrails hanging in my house? They smell bad. Who could possibly live in such a stinking house?"

"My dear friend, I sold the house to you, didn't I? I kept the nail for myself and I told you that I wasn't going to sell it to you. Now, you have no reason to complain."

"Get out of here! I am leaving. I am leaving the house and the money to you. I cannot live here any longer. The stench is overwhelming! The entire house stinks to high heavens."

"If you want to leave the house, be my guest. I have spent all of the money you paid me and I won't give you back one dime," Djeha replied.

"You can keep the house and the money I paid you."

Djeha moved back into his house. The other man started searching for a new home.

Djeha and the Goat Hide

Djeha bought a goat for ten *douros*[12] at the market. He brought it home, killed it, and skinned it.

"This goat was very expensive," he said to his mother.

"Son, what are you going to do with it?"

"For now, let's cook the meat. I'll decide later what to do. The next time we go to the market, we will try to sell the hide. You will come with me and hold the hide. I will circle around you and we will pretend that we don't know each other. I will haggle over the hide, but you will refuse to sell it to me at any price. I will measure it with my hands. You will say to me: 'I'm not selling it.' I will offer you twenty, thirty, forty, fifty, even one hundred *douros*. Among the strangers gathered around us, one will offer you more than that and you will sell it to him. Now, be careful and make sure you stick to the plan."

They went to the market and separated. His mother held the goat hide in her hands. Djeha walked over to her.

"How much have you been offered for this goat hide?"

"Ten *douros*," she answered.

Djeha started measuring it with his hands.

A crowd began to gather around them.

"The hide that you are measuring, what can it possibly be used for?" someone enquired.

"It has many uses. It will become a big drum or a small drum."

Djeha walked away. After a while, he went to his mother and asked her, "Old Mother, how much is your hide going for now?"

"Son, I have been offered twenty *douros*."

"Will you sell it for fifty?"

"No, I won't sell it for that."

Djeha measured the goat hide again with his hands and walked away. People started gathering and telling each other, "Djeha is out of his mind. How can someone so clever fall for something like that?"

Djeha came back.

"Mother, how much have you been offered for that hide?"

"Son, the offer price still stands at fifty *douros*."

"Wait a minute. I will measure it and see if I can use it or not."

He took some time measuring the hide and said to his mother, "I will give you one hundred *douros* for it if you are willing to sell it to me."

"It is not for sale."

Djeha walked away and watched her from a distance. Someone else at the market came and said to Djeha's mother: "Sell it to me. I will give you ten *douros* more for it than that man."

"Quick, give me the money before he shows up again. He might blame me for selling it to someone else."

He handed her the money and she went home. Djeha joined her on the way and they walked home together. The old woman had told the buyer, "This goat hide is very valuable. Put it in the sun. It will dry and you will see what benefit you can reap from it."

The man went home. He put the hide in the sun. Two or three days later, when he went to fetch it, he noticed that it had completely dried out. He picked it up and smoothed it out. The hide split. He went looking for the woman who had sold it to him and found Djeha's mother.

"Old woman, aren't you the one who sold me that goat hide?"

"What did you just say? Do you really believe I sell goat hides? I am Djeha's mother!"

"Well! If that is so, tell me who tricked me if not you."

"Son, I never tricked you."

The man went home thinking she wasn't the seller. He kept the goat hide and fed it to the dogs.

Djeha and His Mother's Shoes[13]

One day, his mother said to him, "I'm leaving to chop some wood." He assumed that she was telling him the truth. She found a nice spot and sat down with her legs crossed. Djeha caught her sitting in the shade cross-legged.

The following day, she said to him, "Son, walking bare-foot is killing me. Go and buy me some shoes, will you?" Djeha bought some cotton and made her a pair of shoes with it.

"Here are your shoes, Mother."

"What are these? How long will they hold up?"

"Mother, if you always work as hard as you did yesterday, they will last you for the rest of your life."

Djeha and the Treasure

When he was a child, Djeha was a bit innocent and igno-rant. With age, he became wiser.

After his father passed away Djeha felt all alone in the world. He only had his mother left. One day, he was going to the market to sell an ox. On his way, he encountered an owl.

"Are you going to buy my ox?" he asked the owl.

The owl hooted in Berber, "Imiârouf!"[14]

"Are you going to give me fifteen reals [gold coins] for it?"

"Imiârouf!" the owl hooted again.

"Are you going to give me twenty?"

"Imiârouf!"

"Are you going to give me twenty-five?"

"Imiârouf!"

"Fine. Here's your ox. And what about the money?"

"Imiârouf!"

"At the next market?"

"Imiârouf!"

"That works for me. Here's your ox. I will come and collect the money from you next time I go to the market."

"Imiârouf!"

Djeha left the ox with the owl and walked home. When his mother asked him what happened to the ox, he said, "I sold it for twenty-five reals. I will collect the money at the market next week."

A week later, on his way to the market, he went to the place where he had left the ox and encountered the hooting owl again.

"What about my money?"

"Imiârouf!"

"I am here to collect my money."

"Imiârouf!"

Djeha walked over to the owl saying, "I really need to collect my money today."

The owl flew to some old ruins. Djeha followed the owl, pleading with it: "You must give me my money!"

"Imiârouf!" the owl hooted.

Djeha followed the owl into the ruins. When the owl flew away, Djeha discovered a treasure hidden in the ruins.

"Do you think that I am a thief like you? I never steal anything. I will only take what is mine."

He took twenty-five reals from the treasure and left.

Back home, he said to his mother, "Mother, the person I sold the ox to is extremely wealthy! I took the twenty-five reals from his treasure myself, I swear!"

"Son, let's go find him."

"Sure, if you want to. . . . But I am afraid that you might steal some of his money."

"Nonsense. Why would I steal something from your friend if we are his guests?"

"Fine, let's go."

She quickly cooked some fava beans, eggs, and crêpes to bring with her. As they were leaving the village, she threw the beans at him. Djeha picked them up and cried out: "Mother, it is raining fava beans!"

"My child, go gather them all," she said. Djeha picked up the beans and ate them. His mother kept on walking. When they arrived at the place where the treasure was hidden, she asked him, "Son, where is your friend's house?"

"It's over there."

"Show it to me, will you?"

"It's over there."

"Is it this one?"

"Come with me, I will show it to you." When they went to the ruins, she found the treasure. She threw the crêpes into the air and made it rain crêpes on Djeha.

"Mother, it is raining crêpes!" He started picking up the crêpes and eating them. Meanwhile, his mother stole the treasure.

"Don't take anything, Mother!"

"I won't, son." While he was distracted, she sneaked off and stole the treasure. She wrapped it in a large towel and carried it away.

"Let's go, my child," she said. They left.

When they arrived at the village, she threw the eggs at him.

"Mother, it is raining eggs!"

He picked them up and ate them. They continued on home. That evening, Djeha went to the *jemaâ*[15] and said, "Today, Mother and I brought home a treasure."

The men at the meeting asked Djeha, "When did this happen?"

"When we left, it started raining fava beans. Then, when it started raining crêpes, we found the treasure and Mother carried it away. And when we came back to the village, it started raining eggs."

"You don't say!"

They talked among themselves.

"This innocent boy doesn't know what he's talking about. Don't believe a word he says, he must be crazy," the counselor said.

Djeha's clever mother had brought along the food that rained from the sky knowing that none of the men would believe Djeha and that the treasure would be all hers.

The Burial of Djeha's Father[16]

The day his father passed away, Djeha took him to the marketplace and buried him there. He left one of the corpse's feet sticking out of the ground. People asked him: "What is this?! Djeha, why are you letting your father's foot stick out of the ground like that? What kind of a burial is that?"

"Everybody knows how to bury their father. This is my father's burial place, all right? When I arrive at the marketplace, I will tie my donkey to my father's foot and there is nothing you can do about that."

One day, Djeha went to the market. He tied his donkey to his father's foot and left to buy and butcher an ox. He bought a skinny ox, killed it, skinned it, cut it up, and put the chunks of meat on a big rock. All of the other butchers were killing fat animals and left when they had sold them all. Djeha stayed put. All of the passers-by spit at him. By nightfall, he was all alone and surrounded by stray dogs.

"Would you like to buy some meat?" he asked the dogs.[17]

They started growling. Djeha said to the leader of the pack, "If you are in charge, tell the dogs that I will sell them my meat."

The dog growled.

"I know that I can get my money from you."

Djeha left and the dogs ate the chunks of meat.

The following day, he went back to the market and headed straight to his father's grave. He noticed that someone had tied their mule to his father's foot.

"Who did this?"

The owner of the mule got up and said, "I did."

"What?! This is my father's grave. I left his foot above the ground so that everybody would know that this is my spot, because you can clearly see that this is my father's grave, and all the people who come here should know that this spot belongs to me and that nobody can go near it."

The owner of the mule apologized, "I didn't know that this was your father's foot. I thought it was a stake."

"Never come here again!"

From that day forward, that particular spot belonged to Djeha.

Djeha Marries a Sultan's Daughter

As soon as Djeha and the owner of the mule parted ways, Djeha went looking for the leader of the pack. When he found the alpha dog, he said, "Now, I want you to give me my money." The dog ran away. Djeha ran after it, saying, "You will not get away with this."

He was planning to use the dogs for a ruse, because one day, he had heard people say that the sultan's daughter had never laughed nor spoken since the day she was born.[18] He had also heard that the sultan had promised to give his daughter to the person who could make her laugh.

Djeha bought a rope and tied it around a tree. Then, he caught all the dogs he could find and tied them up with his rope. As soon as he finished tying them up, he started chasing them with a stick, shouting, "Give me my money!"

The sultan's house faced the tree and the sultan's daughter witnessed the scene from her window. Djeha was making a fool of himself, chasing the dogs to and fro, while they frantically evaded him.

The sultan's daughter burst out laughing, and the servant heard her.

"Your Highness, my mistress is laughing." The sultan rushed to his daughter.

"My daughter, why are you laughing? You haven't laughed since the day you were born. Today, the Lord brought happiness to your heart."

"Father, can you see what this man is doing to the dogs? That's why I am laughing."

The sultan said to his slave, "Go to the man who has caught those dogs and tell him to set them free. Tell him that the sultan is asking him to come."

The servant left and told Djeha to release the dogs and to go to the sultan's palace.

"I will not release the dogs, because I sold them an ox at the last market. When market day came around again, they refused to pay me."

"Come with me to the sultan; don't be crazy! He will make you a rich man, God willing."

Djeha released the dogs, thinking, "Perhaps you are just playing games with me; we will see." He followed the servant and when they had arrived at the sultan's palace, the sultan asked him, "What are you doing to those dogs?"

"Well, I sold an ox to them at the market, and they ate it. Today, I asked them for my money, and they refused to give it to me. That's why I rounded them up."

"How much money do they owe you?"

"Twenty *douros*."

"Follow me," the sultan said. He took Djeha to a room that was filled with money.

"Feel free to take as much as you want."

"That's not what I want. Just let me go so I can catch the dogs that owe me money."

The sultan's daughter was there. She burst out laughing again.

"You are right to mock me, because after I managed to round up all who owe me money, your father tricked me. Your father should have given me your hand, but he only offered me money. He has forgotten his oath. Now, just let me go my way so that I may track down my debtors."

When the sultan saw how dirty Djeha was, he didn't want to give him his daughter's hand. But when Djeha mentioned his oath, the sultan remembered his promise.

"Fine, you may marry my daughter."

"I will not marry her," he said, because he wanted to be treated with respect.

"Why won't you marry her?"

"Because even though, as you can see, I am very dirty, I am a sultan's son. Therefore, treat me the way I deserve to be treated."

"I certainly wish to do so, too. I wanted my daughter to marry a sultan's son, not a peasant."

The sultan gave him his daughter's hand, and Djeha married her.

"Now, my son-in-law, are you going to live in my house or in your house?"

"I won't live in your house. I have a house of my own."

"Fine. Here's your wife; take her. Also, take all the money, all the camels, all the horses, and all the mules that you want."

Djeha took his wife home and became very wealthy.

Djeha and His Wife[19]

Djeha brought his wife home. When she saw the house, she didn't like it one bit. Everything seemed dirty to her.

"What just happened?" she wondered to herself. "This man tricked me! He told me he was the son of a sultan and that he was from an illustrious family and now this! His house stinks to high heaven!" She kept her feelings to herself because she didn't want anyone to know how she felt. When the holidays drew closer, she saw that Djeha was leaving the house to go to work. All the other people had taken the day off because of the celebrations.

"Djeha! Everybody is resting on this holiday, and you are going to work? Didn't you tell me that you are the son of a sultan, that you have a beautiful home and that you come from a wealthy family?"

"My dear, that is true. I told you that and I wasn't lying. I'm going to do some work now."

"Nobody is working, because today is a holiday. We can take the day off because we work hard on all the other days of the year."

"That is true, my dear. However, if the villagers see me not working, they will also stop working. If they see me leaving for work, they will do the same. Now, I can survive without working; I won't lack for anything. I act the way I do in public so that the children of the common people won't be starving."

On another occasion, she asked him, "Djeha, why are you dressed so poorly? Why aren't you dressed like the son of a sultan?"

"My dear, I don't want to wear beautiful clothes because of the commoners. They copy everything I do. For example, if I rest, they also stop working. If I wear beautiful clothes, they will—if they have enough money—buy beautiful clothes for themselves, and then the entire family will go hungry."

"Djeha, how could you tell me you are a sultan? And yet, I have never seen you govern! Also, none of the commoners ever call you 'sultan,' or 'sultan's son.' You lied to me. You are probably just a beggar and a fraud."

Djeha replied, "If that is so, tell me, what are your intentions? If you plan to stay here, don't go crazy. Stay at home. If you realize that you have lost your mind and that perhaps you have had enough of me, then go to your father's house. I don't like lower-class people who think they are better than everybody else. I am the son of a sultan, and I can't do anyone wrong."

"I will only believe that you are a sultan if you kill that muezzin who wakes me up so early every morning."

"I will kill him tomorrow. I will bring you his head and then you will admit that I am a sultan and not an impostor."

Djeha and His Burnous[20]

One day, Djeha and his wife went to the river. While his wife was doing laundry, he was sleeping in the bushes. She washed Djeha's burnous and hung it from a tree branch. The burnous stood up straight as if a man was wearing it. All of a sudden, one of Djeha's enemies appeared. He had seen Djeha and his wife walking to the river and he was planning to shoot Djeha. As he drew closer, he saw the burnous that had been hung up to dry and that was standing up straight. He thought Djeha was standing there and opened fire on the burnous, hitting it and tearing it to shreds. Djeha's wife came running. She started screaming and crying. Djeha woke up and asked her what was the matter with her.

"Somebody just shot at your burnous. Look what he did do to your burnous with his buckshot!" Djeha's wife exclaimed.

Djeha started laughing and dancing.

"Seriously?!" his wife cried out. "You have no heart. Your burnous is in tatters, and you are laughing and dancing!"

"I am laughing and dancing. Why should I be crying?"

"Your burnous has been shredded. How could this possibly not upset you?"

"I am not upset, because if I had been wearing my burnous, the man would have killed me. But since I am alive, I have reason to laugh and dance."

Chapter 2

Animal Tales

In his essay "Why Look at Animals?" British essayist, novelist, and cultural thinker John Berger traces anthropomorphism from Homer, to Aristotle, to Descartes, to Jean-Jacques Rousseau, and then to Claude Lévi-Strauss. Berger notes that "until the nineteenth-century anthropomorphism was integral to the relation between man and animal and was an expression of their proximity. Anthropomorphism was the residue of the continuous use of the animal metaphor. In the last two centuries animals have gradually disappeared. Today we live without them" (1980, 11). Anthropomorphic animal characters abound in Berber folktales. The donkey, called *aghioul* in Berber, is imbued with the most anthropomorphic characteristics. It is Djeha's alter ego (Basset 1920, 31). A Jewish Tunisian proverb suggests that a master and his donkey are alike:

Kif el 'ârf kif el bim!
Like master, like donkey! (Nahum 1998, 67)

In popular fables and folktales, the donkey is represented as a patient, stubborn, and tough character. In traditional

Kabylia, the donkey symbolizes man's sexual power as well as the fertility of the earth that provides food (Servier 1962, 368). And yet, Djeha often gets angry when people compare him to his donkey to make fun of him, as in the tale "The Jackal's Reply" (see Delais 1986, 42). Djeha's sidekick appears in eight of the sixty tales and is the protagonist of the tales "Djeha Wants to Buy a Donkey," "Djeha and His Donkey," and "Djeha and the Man Who Wants to Borrow His Donkey."[1] The donkey is Djeha's constant companion, and therefore very important to him.[2] Djeha either rides his donkey or uses it to carry goods that he buys or intends to sell at the market. This reflects a reality in French Algeria, when donkeys, horses, and mules were used for transportation in cities and in the countryside.[3] Identical Palestinian (see Jayyusi 2007, 51–52) and Egyptian tales suggests that the trickster loves his donkey more than his wife[4]:

> Joha's wife passed away and he didn't shed any tears. Soon after, his donkey died. He wept and was very distressed. One of his friends told him: "This is astonishing! Your wife died and you did not show the same signs of affliction for her as you did for your donkey!" He replied, "When my wife died, the neighbors came and said, 'Don't be sad,' and they swore, 'We'll find you a prettier one.' But when I lost the donkey, no one offered me any consolation at all. Should my grief for him therefore not be deeper?" (Schmidt 2005, 155)

In Kabylia, donkeys are still used for carrying water, wood, and merchandise and as a mode of transportation, especially in remote mountain areas (Haddadou 2000, 152).

However, riding donkeys is considered the least prestigious mode of transportation, and mules are preferred because they are larger and stronger and therefore more useful in the mountains (Dujardin 2005, 37).

In the tale "Djeha and the Thieves" (chapter 5), Djeha lets a gang of four thieves talk him into trading his mule for their donkey and has an argument with his mother, who accuses him of having no common sense. In the tale "Djeha Wants to Buy a Donkey," the trickster goes to the market to buy a donkey but has his money stolen and returns home empty-handed because he refused to utter the symbolically charged formula God willing (inshallah), which "signals the passage from own world to another, which is ruled by a different logic, the imaginary of the future and all its possibilities" (Bourdieu 1977, 27); essentially, the future is ruled by uncertainties and vagaries. In general, the invocation inshallah is used to refer to the future (Ben Danou 1971, 11).

By contrast, the rooster is valued for its symbolic virility and is therefore an animal Djeha identifies with, as in the tale "Djeha and His Friends at the Hammam" (chapter 3), where he reacts to a prank his friends played on him (they sit and "lay" eggs by pulling them out of their clothing) by pretending to be a rooster among hens (his friends). Djeha thus asserts his masculinity and puts his friends in their place, given that hens are "ridiculed for their foolishness" (Nacib 2002, 82). In fact, the Prophet Muhammad recommended that everyone own a rooster, and hence this farm animal enjoys a high reputation in North African society (Bouhdiba 1994, 93). This is because the rooster crows even before the muezzin gets up, thus helping to wake up people in time for the morning prayer. Roosters are often butchered (by having their throats cut) and cooked on special days such as the Day of Ashura (the day of mourning the dead) and at festivities held for the circumcision of boys.

The jackal is the equivalent of the human trickster figure in the animal world. In the tale "Djeha and the Jackal," Djeha makes the mistake of trusting the jackal and invites the predator into his home. But, as the tiger cannot change its stripes, the jackal cannot be domesticated and ends up eating Djeha's son. Similarly, an Algerian saying states, "The clothing is that of a haj (someone who has made the pilgrimage to Mecca, the fifth pillar of Islam), but the gaze remains that of a jackal," meaning that people cannot fundamentally change, nor can they shed their bad habits (Aceval 2005, 151). In North African Berber culture, the jackal is endowed with anthropomorphic trickster qualities: he is called the "jackal with the thousand tricks" (Lacoste-Dujardin 2005, 85). He is by far the cleverest, most streetwise, quickest witted, and most fearsome figure in the animal world, much more so than the wolf or the fox (see Basset 1920, 224). In that sense, the jackal is the equivalent of Djeha in the animal world. Sometimes the jackal is a storyteller, such as Si Mohand, Ben Yakoub, Ben Brahim, or Si Youssef—well-known popular poets, storytellers, or bards (see Nacib 1981, 73; Feraoun 1960). In Berber folktales, the jackal generally even outsmarts the fox, traditionally the cleverest animal in French tales, for instance in the French medieval *Le Roman de Renart*. The Berber jackal is most definitely never to be trusted. It is the Kabyle counterpart to the European wolf that appears in "Little Red Riding Hood" (Perrault's "Le Petit Chaperon Rouge" and the Brothers Grimm's "Rotkäppchen"), as well as in the popular tale "The Wolf and the Seven Little Kids" ("Der Wolf und die sieben Geißlein") also by the Brothers Grimm.

Farm animals and domestic animals (in particular cows, donkeys, goats, horses, mules, and oxen) and wild animals (boars, hyenas, jackals, lions, monkeys, owls, partridges, porcupines, rabbits, ravens, snakes, etc.) frequently appear in Kabyle folktales, highlighting the proximity of humans and wild or domestic animals in remote mountain villages called bleds. Jackals roam so close to Kabyle villages that they have come to symbolize the maquis. This predator is also reputed to have a whimsical, extravagant character, as symbolized by a rainbow that suddenly appears in the sky, which is referred to as "the jackal's wedding." Spotting a jackal in the morning is a good omen (Lacoste-Dujardin 2005, 85). In the trickster tales, the jackal appears to be almost human, on the verge of sociability. But still, like the anthropomorphic wolf in "Little Red Riding Hood," the jackal remains an animal that eats sheep, goats, and sometimes humans, as in the folktale "Djeha and the Jackal," where the trickster makes the fatal mistake of trying to domesticate the predator. Occasionally, the jackal functions as a helper; for instance, in the Berber version of Perrault's tale "Puss in Boots," it is a jackal (or sometimes a monkey) that plays the part of Perrault's trickster cat that helps the miller's son to become wealthy and to marry a princess. As for dogs (see "Djeha and the Dog"), they were traditionally scarce in Kabylia, where it was forbidden to serve dog meat to customers, although some eateries were suspected of doing so. Dogs were reputed to have the same origin as jackals, because both animals refused to be domesticated and preferred to remain wild (Lacoste-Dujardin 2005, 93). Domestic dogs and cats are the objects of indulgent contempt and only tolerated, because they protect the house against burglars or mice (Nacib 2002, 82).[5]

In this collection, some animals are endowed with anthropomorphic qualities or are believed to possess magical powers, such as the talking jackal in the tale "Djeha and the Jackal," and the owl that hoots the onomatopoeic sound "Imiârouf" in the tale "Djeha and the Treasure" (chapter 1). Djeha is convinced that an anthropomorphic owl he thinks is his friend and ally converses with him and therefore gives the owl permission to keep a treasure that he found. Birds also appear quite often in North African folktales, where they function as messengers, facilitators, or helpers on the hero's quest or announce the outcome of his quest. While some birds like vultures are threatening, others like larks or storks are considered friendly. Birds often herald important events. They symbolize the possibility of transformation and symbolically link characters to the otherworld. They occupy an intermediate place between earth and sky, humans and God. Ravens are said to be very cautious; they teach their little ones to beware of humans (Mammeri 1980, xxii). In the tale "The Raven," where the raven steals a bar of soap from his wife, Djeha points out the bird's intelligence to his wife. An identical version of this tale exists in the Orient, only there, it is Nasreddin Hoca's mother who washes their clothes in the yard when a raven steals their bar of soap (see Muzi 2009, 90).

Djeha Wants to Buy a Donkey[6]

One day, he went to the market to buy a donkey. Someone asked him, "Where are you going?"

"I am going to the market to buy a donkey."

"Djeha, you should add, 'God willing,'" the man replied.

"Why would I say 'God willing?' I have money, and there are donkeys at the market."

Djeha left. When he arrived at the market, a man appeared out of nowhere and caught him off guard. He stole all of his money, and Djeha went home empty-handed. He ran into the man again.

"What did you purchase, Djeha?"

"My money was stolen, God willing. May your father be cursed, God willing."

Djeha and the Rabbit Sauce[7]

A farmer brought Djeha a rabbit as a gift. Djeha prepared a fine meal of rabbit for them both. A few days later, someone else knocked at his door.

"Who is it?" Djeha asked.

"I am the neighbor of the man who brought you the rabbit."

Djeha invited him in and gave him something to eat. A while later, another man came and knocked at his door.

"Who is it?"

"I am the neighbor of the neighbor of the man who brought you the rabbit," the stranger replied.

Djeha let him in and served him a glass of warm water.

"What is this?" the stranger asked.

"This is the rabbit sauce you came looking for."

The Raven[8]

One day, Djeha and his wife went to the river to do laundry. While they were washing their clothes, a raven swooped down, stole their soap, and flew away. Djeha's wife started screaming.

"Hush, wife. Let the raven take the soap. It needs the soap to wash its feathers because they are blacker than ours."

Djeha and His Donkey[9]

One day, a man asked Djeha to loan him his donkey.

"Friend, my donkey is not here." Djeha had not finished his sentence when the man heard the donkey bray.

"But I hear your donkey bray, Djeha."

"What?! You'd rather believe the donkey than me, an old man with a white beard?!"

Djeha and the Dog

One day, Djeha saw a dog roaming in the cemetery. When he picked up a stick to hit the dog, the dog lunged at him. Djeha was scared and said to him, "Pardon me, sir, I didn't recognize you."

Djeha and the Man Who Wants to Borrow His Donkey[10]

A man asked Djeha to lend him his donkey.

"Wait, brother. Let me go ask my donkey," Djeha said to him.

He went to the stable and stayed there for a while. When he returned, he told the man, "Brother, my donkey said 'No.'

He is afraid that if I loan him to you, he will be beaten or starved to death and that his master will be cursed."

Djeha and the Two Oxen[11]

Djeha said to his mother, "Now that we sold the goat hide, let's use the money to buy two oxen." He left and bought two oxen for one hundred *douros*.

"Now, what are we going to do with these oxen?" he asked his mother.

"Use them to plow the field."

He left to plow the field. When he had put the yoke on the oxen and started plowing, the plow broke. He took a hatchet, cut the wooden plow, and carried away some long sticks from it.

"Now we will sell these sticks, just like we sold the goat hide."

"Very well," his mother said.

They went to the market. His mother had the sticks. Djeha came to haggle over them.

"Old Mother, how much have you been offered for these pieces of wood?"

"Son, they are expensive."

"Just tell me how much."

"Well, then! I've been offered forty *douros* for them."

"If you want to sell them, I will give you fifty for them."

Then someone asked him, "Djeha, you are willing to pay fifty *douros* for these sticks? Are you out of your mind, or what's the matter with you?"

"What do you know about any of this? If she agreed to sell them to me, I would pay up to one hundred *douros*, because I know how useful it is to have wood for plowing. It is very useful."

Djeha walked away.

The man came and said to the old woman, "Quickly sell them to me for one hundred *douros* before Djeha comes back."

"Give me the money. Hurry up and let me go!"

He paid her and she left. The buyer loaded the lumber and left. Djeha and his mother went home as well.

"Mother, now we still have these oxen. I have to come up with a trick to sell them."

He took an ox and attached a golden coin to its thigh. He also dressed it up in bright colors and took it to the market. A crowd started gathering around him.

"How much do you want for your ox?" someone asked him.

"My ox is expensive, because it produces golden coins."

"Nobody will be able to afford it," someone remarked.

"Many people have enough money to buy it."

"Well, I'll buy it from you," somebody said to Djeha.

"Fine, I'll sell it to you."

"I'll give you fifteen hundred *douros*."

"Son, I cannot sell it at that price."

"Fine, then tell me how much you want for it."

"I won't tell you. Make me a better offer."

"In that case, I will give you two thousand *douros* for it. Take it or leave it."

Djeha sold it to him.

"Djeha, how do I make this ox produce golden coins?" the buyer asked.

"Spread out a rug underneath it for two or three days, and don't worry. Then, feed it some grass so that it may eat its fill. If you do exactly as I say, it will produce golden coins for you."

"Sounds good."

The owner of the ox went home, spread out a rug underneath it and fed it grass. He always found the rug full of cow dung. This went on for two or three days. The man kept washing the rug and putting it back under the animal. After three days, the buyer went back to the market to return the ox to Djeha. Djeha had brought his second ox, made up even prettier than the previous one. Several buyers gathered around Djeha and asked him: "For the love of God, Djeha, what have you done to your ox?"

"My ox sleeps until morning. When it gets up, it is loaded down with golden and silver chains, and it even has golden coins on its thighs."

"Is it for sale?" someone asked Djeha.

"Yes."

The man who had bought the first ox asked him, "Aren't you the one who sold me that ox last time?"

"What do you mean? You don't recognize the person who sold it to you?"

"My dear Djeha, I'm not sure. But it might have been you who sold it to me."

"Well, my friend, it couldn't have been me who sold it to you, because I only have this one ox that I brought here to sell. I've never sold an ox before. I just brought this one here today."

"If that's the case, Djeha, help me find the seller who ripped me off."

"Listen, I'm telling you that I had nothing to sell. Now, please step back and let me do my business in peace. Go find the person who ripped you off. I have nothing to do with it. I am innocent. Leave me alone."

"Sure, I'll leave you alone. I just wanted to ask you a few questions, that's all."

The buyers surrounded Djeha and asked him, "Son, what did he say to you?"

"Just ignore him. If you want to buy the ox, then do so, and don't listen to that fellow."

"We will buy it if you are willing to sell it."

"I brought my ox here to sell it. I didn't bring it for show."

"Well then, if you are willing to sell me your ox, I will buy it. I will give you whatever your asking price is," one person said.

"Fine! I want three thousand *douros* for it."

"Djeha, that's unreasonable. Three thousand *douros* is too much for an ox."

"If you want to buy it, do so. If you choose not to, don't waste my time."

"Djeha, I didn't come to waste anyone's time. I came to buy an ox," the man said.

"If that's the case, then buy it if you want to buy it or else mind your own business."

"I will not give you the asking price, Djeha. I will pay a normal price for it. I will give you two thousand *douros*."

"For God's sake, take your ox and give me the money. Take what belongs to you and let me mind my own business."

Djeha sold him the ox and left. When the buyer was about to walk away with his ox, he called out to him, "Hey, Djeha!"

"What do you want?"

"Come back!"

Djeha returned.

The man asked, "What do I need to do with the ox so that, in the morning, it will get up covered with the golden and silver chains that you talked about?"

"There are not just chains; the ox also produces golden coins. Let me explain what you need to do."

"I'm all ears, Djeha."

"Feed it only green grass so that it may eat its fill, and don't worry about anything."

"May God make you wealthy and bless you!" the buyer said.

Turning to the man who had argued with him earlier and accused him of selling him an ox, Djeha said, "On the next market day, I will bring you a mare that gives birth to a foal every month. As for the ox, son, it wasn't me who sold it to you. I swear on my life that I wasn't trying to trick anybody." He said this to gain the man's trust.

A few days later, the man came back to the market. He really thought that Djeha would bring the special mare. As for the man who had bought the second ox, he brought it back to return it to Djeha. Both men found his market stall empty. They searched the entire market for Djeha but couldn't find him.

They went home feeling betrayed. From then on, Djeha went to other markets to play his tricks.

The High-Strung Horse

Djeha didn't know how to ride a horse, but he was a quick on his feet. One day, the village chief called him and said, "Djeha, I need you to take this letter to the bey of Algiers. Get on my horse and hurry up." The chief's horse was a temperamental horse that nobody could ride, except its master. Djeha, who knew this, managed to avoid the situation by asking, "Is this an urgent matter, master?"

"It is very urgent."

"In that case, I will walk there. I will get there on foot faster than on horseback."

The caid laughed at Djeha's quick-witted reply. He had only been joking with Djeha and didn't expect him to ride the fiery horse. "Sit down and have lunch with the rest of us."

The Rent

Djeha had rented a room in a house. His landlord lived in the same house. Djeha never paid his rent and made a lot of noise in his room all night. One night, the landlord couldn't sleep because of all the ruckus. He asked him: "Why do you make so much noise in your room all night?"

"Son, I train snakes to sell them to the Aïssaouas!"[12]

"You're breeding snakes in my house?! If that is true, I'm ordering you to move out. I won't ask you for any rent if you and your snakes move out today."

"That's exactly what I wanted," Djeha thought to himself. "Let that landlord pay his own rent."

Djeha and the Jackal

Djeha encountered a jackal in the woods.

"Jackal, what is the deal with you? Why do you roam the woods all day and all night? Come on, let's go to my house.

We will live together. You will eat what I eat. We can just hang around together."

"God created me so that I may roam the woods. I cannot possibly be tamed," the jackal replied.

"I just want to do something nice for you!" retorted Djeha.

"You are clever, but I am ten times cleverer than you. You cannot outsmart me."

"My dear friend, I promise not to trick you at all. You have no reason to be suspicious. I would be pleased if you came with me to my house to eat and drink. That's better than roaming the woods, where you are exposed to thorny bushes, cold, and hunger."

"Let me repeat what I just said: you are a great fraudster and so am I. Therefore, the two of us should never get together," the jackal replied.

"And why is that? Are we not brothers? I just felt sorry for you; otherwise, I wouldn't have invited you into my home."

"I've told you, and let me say it again: I shouldn't go home with you. However, since you won't listen to reason, I accept your invitation."

Djeha left with the jackal. When they got home, the jackal said, "I'm not going inside. I will sleep here, on your doorstep."

"Why won't you sleep inside? It's cold outside."

"I want to stay here, because I am used to the cold."

"Fine, stay outside."

The jackal settled down outside and Djeha went inside. When it was dinnertime, Djeha served him his food outside. The next morning, he also fed the jackal outside. This went on until one day, Djeha had to leave. He told his wife to watch out and admonished her not to let their son out of the house because of the dangerous jackal. Djeha was gone a long time. His wife went about her usual business; she didn't notice her son go outside. The jackal saw the little boy and devoured him. The animal carefully licked up all the blood, making sure to leave absolutely no evidence behind. The little boy's mother went outside looking for her son. When she couldn't find him, she asked the jackal if it had eaten her child.

"If that's what you think of me, why did your husband invite me to stay with you? Did I come here to be pestered by your screaming?" the jackal retorted.

Djeha, who arrived at that precise moment, stopped in his tracks when he heard his wife crying. He rushed to her side and asked what was wrong with her.

"That jackal that you brought here has devoured our son!"

Pretending to be angry, the jackal then said to Djeha, "I told you so the very first day: 'Leave me alone, I won't go to your house.' After all, it is you who forced me to come here. Now, may God bless you! So this is how you treat your friends? Now you have to let me go!"

"Please stay and don't pay the slightest attention to what she says," Djeha said.

Djeha went looking for his wife and told her, "I'm telling you to hold your tongue so that the jackal won't leave. As for our son, I too suspect that the jackal ate him. For the time being, let's make sure our guest stays here so that I may avenge the murder of our son."

The jackal knew what was going on. He could sense that Djeha was going to slits its throat once it had fallen asleep. Aware that this might happen, the jackal waited until his hosts had fallen asleep, then jumped over the wall and ran away.

When Djeha and his wife got up the next morning, they realized that the jackal had left.

"The jackal left because of you. If you hadn't yelled so much, it wouldn't have run away and we would have killed it. But after that fit of yours, the jackal had no choice but to escape."

Chapter 3

Faces, Places, or Daily Life in the Village

North African trickster tales revolve around everyday life. They are short literary adaptations of oral folktales that by and large reflect realities described by ethnographers (see Bourdieu 1979; Tillion 1958; Haddadou 2000) and folklorists (see Nacib 1981, 1982, 1986, 2002; Lacoste-Dujardin 2003). In Kabyle mythology, the Berber village is "often portrayed as the stronghold of Berberness" (Aïtel 2014, 175). This is clearly the case in folktales that are anchored in a typical Kabyle village, called *taddart* (Lacoste-Dujardin 2003, 28), which is presented as a site of social, socioeconomic, and religious diversity and marked by random encounters, exchange, and trade. Traditionally, social life in the Djurdjura mountain villages revolved around the fountain—a meeting point for women—and the *jemaâ*, a male assembly or congregation of men held at the "house of men" called *tajamaat* (Lacoste-Dujardin 2003, 28). At the *jemaâ* men discussed all kinds of public issues pertaining to the well-being of the village community, including politics, legal issues, and issues linked to the economy, agriculture, war, and public safety. In keeping with the patriarchal structure of society in French Algeria, women were excluded from participating in these meetings, except if they were directly involved in a lawsuit that concerned them. However, women met daily at the village fountain to fetch water, to gossip, and to discuss more private topics, for instance prospective weddings (Nacib 1981, 96). Traditional Kabyle society was marked by a spatial dichotomy, as women and men occupied separate social spaces:

> The fountain is for the women what the thajm'ath [sic] is for the men. There they exchange news and carry on the gossip which centers essentially on all the intimate matters which the men could not talk about amongst themselves without dishonour, and which they only learn about through their wives. The man's place is outside, in the fields or at the assembly, amongst other men; this is something the young boy is taught very early. A man who stays at home all day is suspect, as is a woman who spends all day outside. (Bourdieu 1979, 23)

The traditional Kabyle mountain economy rested on agriculture, arboriculture, trade, peddling, and various crafts, including wood carving, jewelry making, weaponry, carpet weaving, and pottery (Lacoste-Dujardin 2003, 8). Landownership was (and continues to be) highly desirable. In the tale "Djeha, the Field, and the Old Woman," the trickster uses ruses—*hiyal*—to trick an older woman out of ownership of her family-owned lot. Laws pertaining to landownership in precolonial and colonial Algeria were extremely complex and varied from cities, mountains,

and desert areas. Though French colonial rule was characterized by large-scale expropriations (on this, see Lorcin
1995), in mountain areas exclusive private ownership of
land (referred to as *melk*) existed because, unlike nomadic
or seminomadic desert tribes, the Berbers were sedentary. Yet, landownership was, as Mohamed Hédi Cherif
points out, "always integrated into a communal frame-
work." ([1995] 2004b, 111). Consequently, in a way, Djeha's
ruse to get grass for his donkey is legitimate because it
can be seen as an act of reclaiming rightful land use and
ownership of what historically and traditionally had been
communal land.

The economic importance of livestock farming, agriculture, and trade in these mountain enclaves is evident in
"Djeha and the Miller," where the trickster grinds wheat.
It is also apparent in the numerous tales that take Djeha
to the market, where fruit and vegetables, cereals, medica-
tion, kitchen accessories and household goods, animals,
and many other goods and services can be bought or
traded and where the trickster sells various products, animals, and meat (also see chapter 1, "The Burial of Djeha's
Father," where Djeha butchers a skinny ox at the souk and
stray dogs devour it). Traditional Berber society was characterized by socioeconomic hierarchies and made up of
various professional groups such as artisans, blacksmiths,
barbers, and butchers. Butchers were marginalized by
farmers, who were the proud owners of oxen. The villagers used professional butchers because they were said to
be the direct descendants of African slaves (Servier 1962,
78–79). Another popular place of socialization was the public bathhouse, called hammam, where gender segregation
was strictly enforced (see Jones 2012b).

In the 1930s, while she was on a scientific mission in the Aurès mountains (home to the Chaoui Berber tribe), French ethnographer Germaine Tillion was struck by the "good nature, warm-heartedness and sense of humor" (1958, 15) of the villagers she encountered. During her stay, she noticed the popularity of pranks and practical jokes that recall the trickster from the tale "Djeha and His Watch," where his neighbors play a trick on him while he is asleep. Tillion writes, "Theirs was a fairly well-balanced existence, thanks to the unlimited mutual aid that linked the inhabitants of a village or a group of tents, the pride they all took in this solidarity, the *enormous fun they got out of playing dirty tricks on their neighbors and the relative harmlessness of these pranks*" (1958, 15; emphasis mine). In the absence of modern technology, a host of leisure activities, sports, and other entertainment outlets that exist today, playing tricks or pranks would indeed appear to be a fun pastime.

In most of the tales, Djeha is at the bottom of the social hierarchy in his village, because he is either young, naïve, and uneducated or old and destitute. In the tale "Djeha and the Treasure" (chapter 1), he comes across as a complete idiot, when he "sells" his ox to an owl. However, later on, he accidentally discovers a treasure when he goes back to the woods to demand payment from the owl. As usual, young Djeha is unable to benefit from his unexpected discovery and needs his mother's help to take the treasure home safely. The portrayal of the trickster as an imbecile is quite rare in Berber tales, where he usually purposely acts stupid (see Basset 1920, 173–75). The narrator in "Djeha and the Treasure" attributes his naïvety to his young age and adds that, as he grew up, he became smarter. Still, even as an adult, his existence continues to be a daily struggle for survival.

He strongly resents and despises social hierarchies, rich people, and religious and political dignitaries of all kind, who he feels don't deserve to be wealthy. The tale "Djeha and the Administration" (in Scelles-Millie 2002, 167–73) addresses his contempt of the rich and powerful and the rule of law in general. The trickster is a rebel and an under-dog, an outsider who refuses to let himself be subjugated by anyone.[1] Djeha's laughter is both rebellious and irresistible, and it often functions as a vehicle of relief. His propensity to laugh at his own misery, to effortlessly crack jokes, and to make people laugh even and especially in the face of adversity (such as an oppressive colonial system) provides comic relief and is a quintessential expression of freedom.[2] As humor critic Ron Jenkins writes in his study *Subversive Laughter*, which examines the complex relationship between laughter and freedom, laughter is often a survival strategy: "While colonialism, dictatorship, racism, religious dogma-tism, rigid social conformity, and emotional alienation will never be overcome by humor alone, laughter can play a role in subverting their impact" (1994, 2). In many tales, the trickster's humor expresses dissatisfaction and social criticism. Djeha begrudges the socioeconomic hierarchies in his village, dreams of becoming rich, or of overthrowing the social order. On the other hand, despite his poverty, he wields some authority and is entitled to demand respect on account of his old age, as illustrated in the tale "Djeha and the Local Caid" (chapter 3), where he rebukes the dignitary for sleeping around with pretty women. But even when he calls into question social or socioeconomic hierarchies, he is often humiliated, as in this tale, where he ends up crawl-ing on all fours with a woman straddling him, claiming to be a donkey. In most other tales, however, the trickster outsmarts his various opponents, as in "The Watermelon," which talks about another stock character, the village idiot. In this tale, he steals a watermelon from an orchard (also see "Djeha and the Students," in chapter 5, where he harvests figs from a fig tree that doesn't belong to him, which is a punishable offense).[3]

Djeha and the Miller[4]

One day, Djeha went to the mill to grind wheat. He grabbed his empty straw basket, started collecting the wheat out of the other customers' baskets and filling his own. The miller saw this and asked him, "What are you doing there, Djeha?"

"Don't mind me, I'm just a simpleton."

"If you were an idiot, you would take the wheat out of your own basket and put it in the other people's baskets!"

"I may be an idiot, but if I did that, then I would be a hopeless idiot!"

The miller laughed and let him go.

Djeha and His Friends at the Hammam[5]

One day, his friends decided to take Djeha to the hammam to play a prank on him. They secretly packed some eggs. When they arrived at the hammam, they said, "How about we all lay eggs and whoever can't, has to pay everybody else's admission?"

One of them stood up, started clucking like a hen, and pulled out an egg from underneath him. They all followed suit. When it was Djeha's turn, he got up, started crowing like a rooster, and lunged at his friends. They jumped up and ran away as fast as they could.

"What are you doing, Djeha?"

"What do you think I'm doing? You twenty hens obviously need a rooster."

Djeha and the Qadi[6]

While walking in the countryside, Djeha encountered a qadi (Islamic judge) who was passed out drunk. He stole his coat and walked away. When the qadi woke up, he noticed that his coat had been stolen and sent people to the village to look for it. They found Djeha wearing the coat and escorted him to the judge's house.

"Where did you get that coat?"

"I found a drunken man. I urinated on him and took his coat. If it is yours, take it and forgive me."

"Leave me alone, you crazy man! That's obviously not my coat. I am a qadi, not a drunkard." And Djeha left with the coat.

Djeha and His Jewish Neighbor[7]

Every day, Djeha said the same prayer, "Dear God, give me one thousand dinars [gold coins]. But not a dinar less or else I won't accept the money." One of his neighbors, who was Jewish, overheard him say this every day. One day, his neighbor decided to throw him some gold coins to test him. He threw a purse that contained 999 dinars at him. As soon as Djeha had picked up the purse, he started counting the gold coins and noticed that it was one short of a thousand.

"A generous donor does not mind making a small donation. I praise you Lord and I thank you. You have given me what I asked you for and even if there is a dinar missing, I'll accept it anyway."

Djeha put the money in his trunk. Having overheard everything, the angry neighbor raced to his house and knocked at the door.

"Who is it?"

"It's me."

Djeha opened the door for him.

"What do you want?"

"Give me the money."

"What money? God has given me what I asked him for. There is one dinar missing, but I don't care."

"It's not God that has given you the money. I have thrown it to you in order to test you. Now, enough talking, give me my money back."

They continued arguing.

"Let's settle this matter in court."

"I am old. I can't walk. Let me ride on your donkey," Djeha replied.

"Fine." He loaned Djeha his donkey.

"I'm freezing to death. Let me borrow your coat."

"That's fine," his neighbor said, and he also let him borrow his coat.

They went to court. When they were standing in front of the qadi, the neighbor said to the magistrate, "With all due respect, Your Honor, this man owes me 999 dinars." And he told the judge the whole story.

"Is this true?" the judge asked Djeha.

"He is lying. He always lies. I bet he'll say that this donkey and this coat are his, too."

"Yes, Your Honor. The donkey and the coat are mine; I let him borrow them."

"Get these two jokers out of here," the qadi said to the bailiff. The neighbor left confused.

Djeha kept the money, the donkey, and the coat.

Djeha and the Local Caid

The caid[8] was known to be a womanizer. Djeha, who visited him often, lectured him, "How is it that you, a caid, cannot get enough of women? Control yourself. Fear the Lord. You should be ashamed of yourself!" These words deeply affected the caid, who had a beautiful woman as a servant. She noticed that her master was melancholy and asked him what was wrong with him.

"Djeha called me a womanizer," he replied.

"That's all? Well then, allow me to pay him a visit. Meanwhile, you stay here and then you will pay him a surprise visit. Just wait and see what I will do to him. You will love the state in which you will find him."

"Go now," the caid said to her.

She left and made herself comfortable in Djeha's house. As soon as he laid eyes on her, Djeha fell desperately in love with her. He drew closer to her. She drew back. He followed her. Wherever she sat down, he sat down next to her.

"Stay where you are, Djeha. Don't come near me. If you want to come near me, let me climb on top of you and straddle you. You will walk on all fours with me riding on your back."

"Come here." She saddled and bridled him, and climbed on his back, straddling him. Djeha started walking on all fours when the caid dropped in unexpectedly.

"Djeha, you won't let me love women, but look at yourself now!" the caid exclaimed.

"Your Honor, I was only trying to prevent you from turning into a donkey like me!" The caid burst out laughing and rewarded him handsomely.

Djeha and the Barber[9]

Djeha had his head shaven because he had ringworm. After the barber had finished shaving him, Djeha paid him half of what he owed him.

"Why are you only paying me half?"

"Look, I have ringworm. I only have half the hair."

The Watermelon

One day, his mother said to him, "Son, we are penniless. I won't be able to cook dinner tonight and we will go to bed hungry!"

"Don't worry, Mother. I will bring you a golden coin [louis d'or] today."

Djeha went outside, stole a watermelon from his neighbor's garden, and took it to the market. On his way, he encountered the village idiot riding a mule.

"Good afternoon, sir. That's a fine mule you have there."

"I'd much rather have a mare!"

"You can have a mare for just one golden coin."

"And just how would I manage that?"

"I was on my way to the market to sell this mare's egg," Djeha continued, pointing at the watermelon. "If you want to buy it, I will give it to you for just one louis."

The idiot took a golden coin out of his wallet and gave it to Djeha, who handed him the watermelon. Djeha headed home happily rubbing his golden coin.

The man rode away, proudly clutching the watermelon under his arm. At some point, the mule tripped and the man dropped the watermelon. It rolled into a ditch and split into pieces near a bush where a sleeping hare lay. The hare sprung up and scurried away. The idiot cried out, "Oh no, there goes my newly hatched foal!"

Djeha and His Watch[10]

One day, Djeha was asleep on his rooftop terrace. One of his neighbors called up to him, "Hey! Djeha!" Djeha got up and looked down at him from far up on the terrace.

"What do you want?"

"Come down here, my friend. I need to tell you something."

Djeha climbed all the way down and asked him again, "What do you want?"

"What time is it?" his neighbor asked.

"Follow me up to the terrace."

They both climbed up to the terrace, and Djeha said to him, "My watch broke a week ago. I don't know what time it is."

"Why didn't you tell me that when I was down there?"

"And you, why didn't you ask when I was up here?"

Djeha, the Field, and the Old Woman

One day, Djeha took his donkey to a lush green field. There was an old woman guarding the field.

"Old Mother, will you let me cut some grass for my donkey?"

"I can't let you do that; my children would object."

"Then sell me a little bit of grass from the edge of the field."

"Fine. Cut some off the edge, but don't touch the field."

Djeha gave her a small amount of money. As soon as she took the money, he went to the middle of the field and cut all the grass, destroying the field.

"Didn't I tell you not to go out in the field?"

"So what?"

"You've wrecked the field!"

"I've bought the field."

"Who did you buy it from?"

"From you."

"Take your money back."

"I cannot do that because I already paid you. If you claim otherwise, swear to me that I didn't give you any money and I will leave the field."

She left and returned with her son.

"Djeha, what have you done?"

"I didn't do anything."

"Excuse me? You found my old mother guarding the field. You came and tricked her. You told her, 'Let me cut a bit of grass from the edge.' She let you cut some grass and you claimed that you bought the whole field."

"I paid your mother. If I hadn't, she would not have let me go into the field. Since I've bought the field from your mother, I won't take any orders from either of you."

"Follow me, let's go ask the judge," the old woman's son said. "I refuse to take matters into my own hands."

"Be my guest," Djeha replied.

They went to the courthouse. When they arrived, the son said to the qadi, "Your Honor, this man encountered my old mother and asked her for some grass for his donkey. My mother refused to give him any. He said to her, 'Sell it to me.' 'Fine,' my mother said, 'I will sell you some, but don't go out in the field.' She took the money he gave her and he walked right into the middle of the field."

"My dear friend, this conversation is useless. This is what really happened, Your Honor. I gave her the money. I bought the field. Now, the moment someone buys something and another person comes out of nowhere to take the goods away from that person, there is no need to argue."

"Who did you buy it from?" the qadi asked.

"I bought it from his mother. If a father or mother sells something to someone and their son wants to take it back, now would we let that happen?"

"Perhaps you didn't buy anything at all. She might have let you cut grass out of sheer kindness," the qadi replied.

"Bring her in; make her swear that I didn't give her any money, and I will give her back the field. Otherwise, the field that I bought belongs to me."

Turning to the old woman's son, the qadi said, "Since your mother sold the field, it's settled."

"God bless you, qadi," he replied. "Since it was a woman who made the sale, I don't have any other option but to accept it. I most certainly will run into Djeha again at the courthouse in the future."

"What?" the judge asked. "Your mother made the sale, and you wish to exercise your right of withdrawal?

Your mother brought you into this world, didn't she? Everything she does has consequences for you as well as for your brothers."

"Thank you, Your Honor. I'm leaving."

The son went home and Djeha returned to the field. The sons of the old woman ambushed him and tried to kill him. Djeha escaped; they failed to catch him. He left the area altogether and settled in another part of the country. Later, when he went back to the field, he brought several people with him. Finally, after he had cut and taken all the grass, leaving the ground barren, he told the old woman's sons, "Have your field back. Do what you want with it. I just wanted the grass."

"Now, since you have taken the grass, you might as well take the land, too."

"I don't want the land. I just wanted the grass, and I took it. Take back your property. I don't even live here anymore. I only left this village because you threatened to kill me."

Djeha and His Rope

One day, a student came to Djeha and said to him, "Djeha, loan me your rope so that I can hang some salted meat on it."

"I have a rope that my wife used to dry some couscous."

"Can couscous be dried on a rope?"

"Of course not, but what do you expect me to say? I have to say nonsense like that so that people like you stop trying to borrow my stuff all the time."

Chapter 4

Foodways

Foodways make up a large portion of these folktales. In many tales, the trickster is on the brink of starvation. He is constantly either trying to figure out how to steal food from people or looking for free food, which he then gobbles down ("The Roasted Kid"). He gets desperate or mad when he sees people eating without inviting him to join them ("Djeha and the People Who Were Eating"). He is willing to cheat and lie to others ("Djeha and the Arab") and even to his own father ("Djeha and the Sheep's Head") to either get free food or hide the fact that he was a glutton and indulged in a delicious meal without sharing. While he deliberately breaks the key rule of hospitality (see chapter 5), the opposite does not hold true, since he expects others to share food with him and gets mad if they don't ("Djeha and the People Who Were Eating"). Djeha is so destitute that even his cookware has holes in it ("Djeha and the Pot") or he does not own proper cookware, as in the tale "Djeha and the Owner of the Pot," where he borrows cookware from his neighbor. Much to the neighbor's delight, the pot miraculously begets another pot after Djeha returns it. This highly popular tale featuring either a pot or a pan appears in countless variants around the globe, such as in an Egyptian Goha collection (Finbert 1929, 43–45). The stainless steel, cast-iron, or copper pot is a staple feature in North African folklore. It is endowed with anthropomorphic qualities as the following Berber saying illustrates:

Anta tugwi ur nefrih, anta tugwi ur neqrib?
What pot has never had happy or sad feelings?

The pot stands for the human belly, which is either empty or full. The metonymic figure of the pot is a key element of everyday life, a witness to good times and bad times. For instance, the couscous served at funerals is similar to that eaten on happy occasions such as weddings, circumcisions, and engagements (Nacib 2002, 143).

The trickster's daily struggle for survival and his obsession with securing food and nourishment reflects social realities in colonial French Kabylia. The rude conditions of daily life can be summed up in three terms: a dense population, poverty, and the geographical isolation of the villagers (Nacib 1982, 2). As French ethnographer Germaine Tillion writes in her study *Algeria: The Realities* (published in 1958—in the middle of the Algerian War of Independence), "Algeria is as impoverished as it is immense, and there are enormous disparities in the people's level of development" (3). Algerian folklorist Youssef Nacib concurs with her assessment, stressing that Kabyle villages under French colonial rule suffered from constant food shortages, and the sumptuous meals mentioned in folktales, such as couscous (also referred to as *seksou*), garnished with plenty of meat, are far removed from the historical realities of the time period spanning the French colonization of Algeria

(1830–1962). A typical daily diet consisted of cereals (e.g., wheat, barley, and sorghum), various fruits (e.g., figs), and vegetables. Kabyles usually didn't eat or drink anything before daybreak. Breakfast, the first meal, eaten soon after sunrise, usually featured heated leftover couscous, sometimes figs, and sometimes only bread taken with either milk or water (Mouliéras 1892, 143). Lunch—called *imekli*—was eaten at around eleven o'clock. It consisted of figs or bread (served with water, milk, or whey protein). Only wealthier people ate couscous with lamb meat. Finally, the afternoon snack, a meal of figs and bread, called *thanalt*, was taken at four in the afternoon (Mouliéras 1892, 143). Larger meals, such as the dish in the tale "Djeha and the Meat," were served on special occasions, in particular weddings, circumcision ceremonies, and various holidays such as Aïd Al Adha. "Djeha and the Meat" is almost an exact replica of the French medieval fabliau "The Partridges." In this thirteenth-century tale, a peasant's wife devours two partridges that her husband had ordered her to cook, and when he wants to see them, she claims—as in the Djeha tale—that they were eaten by a cat (see Micha 1989, 50–53). Variants of the tale "Djeha and the Meat" exist in Sephardic Jewish tradition ("Cat or Fish?" in Koén-Sarano 1993, 126–27), in Palestinian (see Jayyusi 2007, 20), and in Tunisian folklore. In a popular Tunisian variant, the trickster's wife eats all the meat herself without sharing it with her brother. The trickster weighs the cat and concludes that his wife lied to him, because the cat is too light: "And if it's the cat [that ate it], where is the meat? And if it's the meat, where is the cat?" (Bouhdiba 1994, 11).

Traditional meals in the villages of the Djurdjura mountain range featured flat cakes (called galettes in

French), couscous made of barley, figs, olive oil, and various seasonal vegetables and fruit (Nacib 1982, 10). These food items were sometimes eaten with chicken, beef, or mutton. After the conquest of Kabylia and the Djurdjura mountain range in 1857, the cultivation of potatoes was introduced in Kabylia (Lorcin [1995] 2014, 83). A popular dessert pastry with honey and dates is called *makrout*. Fig trees (called *taneqqelt*) and olive trees (called *azemmour*) were important sources of nourishment as well as other fruit trees (pear, apple, plum, pomegranate, quince, almond, apricot, cherry; see Dujardin 2003, 34). In fact, both fig trees and olive trees were protected by law against theft and damage, underlining the sociocultural importance of these trees in Berber society (Henri Basset 1920, 95). Figs appear in two tales: "The Turnips" (chapter 4) and "Djeha and the Students" (chapter 5). Figs represent the feminine and symbolize generosity, abundance, and fertility (Bouhdiba 1994, 69). Hence, the suggestion made to Djeha by his friend to present the Islamic judge with figs instead of turnips implies some sexual innuendo (i.e., male impotence) that explains the dignitary's angry reaction. Fava beans (see chapter 1, "Djeha and the Treasure") also carry a sexual symbolism linked to fertility and were part of a ritual aimed at determining whether the harvest would be good. For example, on New Year's Day, the Berber tribe of the Beni Snous used to prepare a meal called *cherchem*, a ritual dish containing fava beans, wheat, and chickpeas. Swelling grains indicated a good year (Doutté 1909, 547). Fava beans are often mentioned in trickster tales, where they can symbolize happiness or be linked to childbirth (see Ben Danou 1971, 178). In keeping with the importance of hospitality[1] in the Maghreb (see chapter 5), guests or visitors were offered foods that ordinary villagers would normally only eat on special occasions, including meat, eggs, pancakes, poultry, and various pastries. Eggs (see the tale "The Eggs") and meat were highly valued because they were reputed to be particularly nutritious and fortifying. They were, in fact, believed to bring the moribund back to life (Nacib 1982, 10).

Djeha and the Chicken[2]

A man once invited Djeha over for lunch. When he arrived, the head of the household served him a roasted chicken. Djeha drank the broth but couldn't eat the chicken because it was old and stringy.

The following day, the same thing happened again. Djeha was served chicken that was too stringy to eat, so he just ate the broth. Then, he grabbed the chicken, placed it facing Mecca and proceeded to do his prayers[3] over the poultry.

"What are you doing there, Djeha?"

"I'm praying over this chicken, because its flesh is surely that of a saint or a prophet. How else could it have gone into the fire twice and come out unharmed?"

Djeha and the Meat[4]

One day, Djeha bought three pounds of meat, gave it to his wife, and asked her to cook him a nice lunch. He went outside while his wife prepared the meat. She and her brother ate all the meat. Djeha came home and saw that there was no meat. He asked what happened to all the meat.

"I was busy cooking when the cat came and ate it."

Djeha got up, lifted the cat, and put it on a scale. He noted that it weighed three pounds.

"Nonsense! If this is the meat, where is the cat? And if this is the cat, where is the meat?"

The Roasted Kid[5]

One day, Djeha had lunch at someone's house. The head of the household served him a young roasted kid. Djeha grabbed the animal and started devouring it like an ogre.

"You are so enraged against this kid, one might think that your mother used to poke you with goat horns," his host said.

"And you are eating too slowly. You appear to feel sorry for it, as if its mother had been your wet nurse."

Djeha and the People Who Were Eating[6]

One day, he walked by a group of people who were enjoying a meal. He said to them, "May God's judgment be kind to you, you greedy people."

"By God, we are not uncharitable," they replied.

"Dear Lord, tell me that I'm the one lying, not them!"

Djeha and the Bread[7]

One day, he was traveling with a group of people. His companions bought loaves of bread and sat down for lunch. Djeha said to them, "My children, I cannot eat a whole loaf of bread by myself. Why don't each one of you take one loaf of bread and give me half of each loaf. That's all I can eat."

Djeha and the Owner of the Pot[8]

One day, Djeha went to one of his neighbors and asked him to loan him his pot so he could cook with it. The neighbor loaned it to him. The next day, Djeha returned the pot. He had put a small pot inside the larger pot.

"Here's your pot." After the neighbor took it, he discovered the smaller pot inside.

"What is this?"

"Your pot gave birth to it."

"Fantastic," the neighbor said and took both pots.

A while later, Djeha went back to the same neighbor and asked him to loan him the pot again. He gave it to him and Djeha kept it. The next day, the neighbor went to Djeha and wanted his pot back. Djeha said, "No, I can't give you your pot back. It's dead."

"What are you talking about? A pot can't die!"

"You've already accepted that it gave birth. Anything that gives birth also must die. And your pot is very dead."

Djeha and the Arab[9]

Djeha was hungry and went for a walk in the countryside. He saw an Arab who was eating and hoped that he would be invited to share the meal. As he approached him, the Arab asked him, "Where are you from, my brother?" He, however, did not invite Djeha to eat.

"I'm from the same village as you."

"If so, I assume that you are the bearer of good news?"

"I'll bring you all the good news you want to hear."

"Do you have any news from our village?"

"Yes, I do."

"Do you have any news from my wife Omm Othman?"

"Oh!" Djeha exclaimed. "She has been prancing about like a peacock!"

"And how is my son Othman?"

"He usually plays marbles with his friends."

"How is the camel doing?"

"It's so fat that it is about to burst."

"Do you have any news of our dog, T'it'ouh'?"

"T'it'ouh' is very mean and that's an understatement. Burglars don't come near your compound; that dog is terrifying."

"And my house is in good shape?"

"Your house is a fortress."

The Arab continued eating in silence. Djeha decided to leave because he was not invited to eat.

"Where are you going, brother?"

"I am going back to the village. Since the day T'it'ouh' died, your house has been swarming with burglars."

"T'it'ouh' is dead?"

"Yes."

"How did my dog die?"

"It died from eating too much camel meat."

"So the camel died as well?"

"Yes," Djeha answered.

"What happened?"

"It tripped over Omm Othman's grave."

"My wife Omm Othman is dead?"

"Yes."

"How did she die?"

"She died of a broken heart after losing Othman."

"My son Othman is dead, too?"

"Yes."

"How did he die?"

"Your fortress of a house collapsed on him and crushed him."

When he heard these words, the Arab rose like a madman and headed toward the village, leaving the food behind. Djeha chuckled to himself as he finished his meal.

The Turnips

One day, Djeha brought the caid some pomegranates. The caid enjoyed the gift. Later, Djeha was going to bring him some turnips, but a friend told him that it would be better to offer him figs instead of turnips. Djeha took his piece of advice. He filled a basket with figs and went to the caid's house. When he gave him the figs, the caid got angry. He refused to take them and ordered the court bailiffs to throw the figs at Djeha's head.

"Thank you and may God have mercy on your father, my friend," Djeha repeated over and over.

"Why are you thanking me?" the caid asked.

Djeha told him exactly what had happened and added, "I was on my way to bring you turnips. But, because of my friend's advice, I brought you figs instead. If I had brought you turnips, my head would already have been shattered into one hundred pieces." The caid smiled at him and rewarded his ingenuity with a gift.

Djeha and the Ewe's Head[10]

One day, his father gave him one franc to buy an ewe's head. Djeha bought the head and gnawed every single piece of flesh off of it. All that was left was a completely clean skull, which he took to his father.

"What is this?" his father asked.

"It's an ewe's head."

"You're kidding me. Where are its ears?"

"It was deaf."

"And its eyes?"

"It was blind."

"Where is the tongue?"

"It was mute."

"And the skin?"

"It was nothing but scabs."

The Eggs

One of Djeha's foes was an egg seller. One day, Djeha met him at the market.

"These are some very nice-looking eggs."

"Enough joking. If you want to buy some do so; otherwise, beat it."

Djeha bought two eggs and carefully slid a golden coin in each one of them. Then he said to his foe, "Listen, I want to make peace with you now and, bearing that in mind, I will give you a good piece of advice."

"Speak, I'm all ears."

"Don't sell these eggs," Djeha whispered into his ears. "They contain golden coins."

"Get out of here, liar!"

"You think that I am lying? Well then, look at this," Djeha said and cracked the two eggs he had bought right in front of him.

The egg seller was stunned when he saw two golden coins emerge from his eggs. Djeha picked them up, put them in his pocket, and went home. The seller immediately took his eggs and cracked them all. He didn't find any golden coins and started cursing, "May God put out Djeha's eyes just like I cracked all of my eggs!"

Chapter 5

The Intricacies of Hospitality: Beware of Friends and Foes!

Hospitality is of the utmost importance in North Africa and the Middle East. It is equally important in Islam and Judaism. André Nahum (1921–2015), a Jewish Tunisian writer and author of several books about Ch'hâ, recounts the stories that he heard from his grandmother, an illiterate widowed young woman called Mâ'ha. In one of his folktale collections, Nahum elaborates on the importance of hospitality:

Hospitality is, as we know, an absolute duty among Jews and Arabs, regardless of their financial means. In the Orient, guests are entitled to everything. The day before *Pessah* [Passover], for instance, during the *seder* [dinner ritual on the eve of the *Pessah*], the front door stays open, so that, as is stated in the *Haggada* [story of the exodus from Egypt that is read during the *seder*], "whoever is hungry can come eat and every poor person can come and celebrate Pessah with us!" (1998, 36)

According to a popular Tunisian proverb, "Hospitality comes first (before your father)" (Nahum 1998, 36). Throughout the Maghreb, hospitality, which entails providing shelter and sharing food, is paramount. Hospitality is

> a link, a contract that binds both parties, because crossing the doorstep and entering a house implies accepting the rules of the house and submission to the ruling authority. This is why a stranger would not be able to go everywhere. . . . Accepting to welcome a host (referred to as *inebgi*) implies placing him (or her) under the protection of the *assass* [guardian of the household] and granting that person food and shelter. (Lacoste-Dujardin 2005, 177)

Traditionally, Berber housewives had to be prepared to provide shelter and cook food for guests at all hours of the day and night and to regale them with basic foods and ingredients, such as semolina, oil, dried meat, and dried vegetables (Nacib 2002, 64). In Islam, the hospitality of the Prophet Muhammad is said to last for three days (Melchert 2015, 71), the implication being that after three days, it is acceptable to ask a guest to leave. The hospitality motif appears in the tale "Djeha's Hare" (chapter 5), where Djeha asks his mother to butcher a rabbit and serve it to their guests. His guests are thieves, and he intends to play a trick on them. In a Tunisian variant of this tale, "The Mice," the trickster catches two mice that he claims are messengers he can send home any time he wants his mother to prepare food. He then sells the supernatural mice at the market. Of course, they turn out to be just ordinary mice, but meanwhile Djeha has tricked the buyers out of money and can buy food (see Nahum 1998, 173–76). In Kabylia, hospitality is closely tied to the concepts of self-respect, honor, and the concept of lifting the gaze, referred to as *qabel*: "An honorable man is a man who faces up (*qabel*), who confronts others by looking them in the face; it also means to receive someone as a guest and to receive him well, to do him honour" (Bourdieu 1979, 128). Under the colonial administration, Berbers were obligated to serve their visitors, usually French diplomats or dignitaries, sumptuous meals or feasts known as *diafa* (also spelled *dhifa* or diffa). An example of this custom appears in the tale "Djeha at the Feast," which suggests that the obligation to produce huge amounts of high-quality food represented a burden for the local population in French Algeria: "As visitors were occasional and their stay but brief, this placed no great burden to the tribe. However, once French rule was established in the High Plateaux, the diffa became an entitlement rather than a freely offered gesture of hospitality.[2] Visiting French dignitaries came to expect it as a matter of right, and the costs rose exponentially" (Burke 2014, 46). In this context, the hosts' reluctance to serve Djeha—who is not a dignitary—delicious food makes more sense.

Mouliéras's trickster collection features a number of connected tales illustrating tale type 968, "Miscellaneous Robber and Murder Stories." In traditional Berber society, theft was in fact part of a ritual game especially among rivaling groups of men (Servier 1962, 67). These particular tales are "various tales dealing with robbers and murderers as characters. In numerous tales, robbers are cheated by the clever actions of a girl (other person)" (Uther 2004, vol. 1, 605). In these tales, Djeha tricks thieves out of money by selling them supposedly magical animals or objects, such as oxen that defecate gold, a pickax that finds food, a knife that brings dead people back to life, and hares that are able to deliver messages. As expected, all of these objects and animals have no magical qualities whatsoever but cause substantial, sometimes irreversible damage to the gullible buyers. In the tale "The Hosts' Pickax," for example, Djeha sells his guests a supposedly magical pickax that can find delicious meals in the ground. As expected, the pickax finds nothing at all, but the thieves destroy their houses while searching the ground for food. In the tale "Djeha and the Thieves," Djeha gets his own back by convincing the four thieves who talked him into trading in his mule for a donkey that his donkey produces golden coins. In North African folklore, the donkey symbolizes the anus and defecation, as well as sadomasochist aspects related to a society that is obsessed with cleanliness and keeping the anus clean (see Bouhdiba 1994). The conceptual link between defecation (by the donkey) and human desire for wealth (in the shape of gold coins) is that they are both morally reprehensible since the desired wealth is not earned fair and square by physical labor (other than feeding the donkey fresh grass).

Djeha masters the art of scheming, hatching projects, and looking extremely busy while in fact being idle. In this respect, he is a rebel, if not a social outcast. He undoubtedly has learned these skills from his mother, who is also reluctant to work (see "Djeha and His Mother's Shoes" in chapter 1). He sometimes works, but he only does the bare minimum to make a living, even though hard work is necessary to climb the social ladder. In his long discussion on happiness, social standing, and wealth in *The Muqaddimah*, fourteenth-century Tunisian historian Ibn Khaldun notes:

A person who has no rank, even though he may have money, acquires a fortune only in proportion to the labour he is able to produce, or the property he owns, and in accordance with the efforts he makes to increase it. This is the case with most merchants and, as a rule, with farmers. It is also the case with craftsmen. If they have no rank and are restricted to the profits of their crafts, they make only a bare living somehow fending off the distress of poverty. (1969, 306–7)

This description reflects Djeha's socioeconomic condition as someone who is marginalized in society because he likes leisure and pleasure (carpe diem) and refuses to work. Instead, he sometimes resorts to unorthodox measures, such as lying and theft to get food. On occasion, the trickster kills animals (oxen and sheep that he sells at the souk) and even humans (the muezzin in "Djeha and the Sheep's Head," chapter 6). On other occasions, he incites other people to kill so that he may keep their money (see "Djeha's Knife Kills and Resuscitates" in chapter 6, where the thieves kill their own wives, because they are so gullible that they believe that Djeha's knife can administer punishment by killing and subsequently resurrecting from the dead). As Pierre Bourdieu pertinently notes, Djeha's numerous allusions to Allah/God in various tales, in formulations such as God willing, if God permits, or if I please God (often used with a hefty dose of self-irony by Djeha after he experienced a mishap), "indicates that one is moving into a different world, governed by a different logic, the unreal world of the futures and possible" (1979, 15) and that God's generosity can be implored but not necessarily be counted on. Reversely, according to a Kabyle saying, "A generous man is God's friend" (Bourdieu 1979, 19). Therefore, being generous implies pleasing God, who in turn might (or might not) show his generosity at harvest time or during other potentially life-changing events such as childbirth. As for Djeha, he can only count on his wits to survive. While he mostly pretends to be a practicing Muslim by submitting himself to Allah's will, he sometimes (see "Djeha Wants to Buy a Donkey," chapter 2) refuses to use invocations to God.

Djeha and His Friends

Djeha's friends paid him a visit because they had heard that he was sick in bed. They were talking so loudly that Djeha couldn't sleep. Exasperated, he got up, grabbed his pillow, and said, "You all can go now. I have been cured. God himself has healed me."

Djeha and His Guests

Djeha was preparing a meat stew when two of his friends showed up. One of them took a chunk of meat and said, "This meat could use some salt." The other friend also picked up a slice of meat and said, "This meat could use some vinegar." Djeha picked up the meat that was left and told them, "This stew could use some meat."

Djeha and His Two Friends

One day, Djeha and his two friends brought home two ewes and a sheep that they had bought at the market. "Djeha, how are we going to split up these animals?"

"You two take one of the ewes and the sheep and I will take the other one."

Djeha and the Burglar[3]

One night, a burglar broke into Djeha's house, stole some of his possessions, and left. Djeha got up, gathered the rest of his personal belongings, and followed the intruder. When the burglar looked back over his shoulder and saw Djeha following him carrying bundles of his possessions, he called out to him, "Hey, man! What do you want?"

"Allah! Allah! We are moving out of our house and into yours. You carry that half of the stuff, and I will carry the rest. Tomorrow, God willing, at the crack of dawn, my wife and kids, my whole family will move into your house. They will be so happy to get out of our shack!"

"Take back all of your stuff and go home. Stop following me, I don't want to deal with your problems," the burglar replied.

Djeha at the Feast[4]

People didn't know what to do to get rid of Djeha; he was such a freeloader. One day, the village elders were going to someone's house for a feast. They arrived with Djeha in tow and wondered, "What are we going to do about Djeha, who always eats all the food?"

Someone suggested, "As soon as the food starts coming, let's tell him that there is a fire in his village. That way, he won't get any of the food. He won't be able to eat because he will be worried about the fire."

When the food came, they said to him, "Djeha, there is a fire in your village."

"Is my house on fire?" Djeha asked.

While they were discussing how to answer him, Djeha quietly started eating.

They said, "Your house is burning down!"

Taking another bite, he asked, "But I'm not on fire, am I?"

"Now your clothes are on fire!!"

"But my head isn't on fire yet, is it? May the fire burn my feet but not my head."

Djeha was still eating. When the others wanted to start eating, they discovered that Djeha had eaten all of the food. "Djeha has tricked us again!"

Djeha Feeds the Students⁵

One day, Djeha was at home with his mother. Since they had nothing to eat, he said to her, "You wait here, while I'll go get us something to eat." He went to a group of students and said, "Follow me, lunch is on me today."

Djeha, who was also a student, had not gone to school that day. When he invited them to his house for lunch, they said, "But Djeha, you are poor!"

"It is customary for students who have memorized the Qur'an to feed their fellow students," Djeha replied.

"Fine. Then go and prepare lunch; we're coming."

"Follow me, lunch is ready."

They got up and went with him. When they arrived at his house, Djeha ushered them into a bedroom. He picked up the shoes that they had left at the door and put them in a bag. He went back to the students, told them he would return shortly, and left with the bag that was filled with their shoes. He went to a restaurant and said to the owner, "Give me something that's worth two francs and take this pair of shoes as payment."

Afterward, he went to a butcher and to a couscous vendor and told them the same thing. After trading all of the students' shoes, Djeha went home, loaded down with plates of delicious food, and served the students a good lunch.

When they were about to leave for school, they couldn't find their shoes. Djeha said to them, "Come with me; I have hidden your shoes."

He took the students to the restaurant.

To the first student, he said, "Give the owner two francs, and he will give you your shoes."

Finally, he showed them all the places where he had pawned their shoes. The poor students had to buy their own shoes back. Djeha returned to his mother. With all the leftovers, they had enough food to eat for two days.

Djeha and the Students

The students wanted to get even for the trick he had played on them. One day, when they were all gathered together, they decided to call Djeha and ask him to pick some figs for them.

"Where is the fig tree?" Djeha asked.

"It's over there," they said.

"I will pick some figs for you."

The students figured that Djeha would take off his shoes when he climbed the tree to get the figs. They intended to steal and sell his shoes to get even with him. When he was about to start climbing, Djeha took off his shoes and stuck them under his armpits.

"Hey! Djeha! What are you doing? You are taking your shoes with you? Leave them here until you get back down."

"A path up the tree might miraculously appear. In that eventuality, I will need my shoes. As for you, poor students, you can steal my shoes some other day. Today is not your lucky day."

Djeha and the Thieves

One day, Djeha went to the market with a mule that he had inherited from his father. It was a very tall mule. He climbed up onto his mule and rode it to the market, where he encountered four thieves with a donkey.

"Djeha, what are you doing? You are riding a mule! Are you out of your mind? One of these days, you will fall off that mule and die. Come here, we will trade you our donkey for your mule. It is short, so if you fall, you won't die."

"By God, you are right."

"What else will you give us?"

"I thought that I'd just have to give you my mule," Djeha said.

"What! You won't give us anything else? We are trying to help you but you won't make a deal with us. We are afraid that you may fall off your mule and die, and then good-bye, Djeha."

"Then tell me how much more I should give you."

"Give us an additional one hundred *douros*. For the love of you, we will be satisfied with that."

"Deal. Bring me that donkey and take the mule."

After they had made the exchange, Djeha left to buy a cooking dish at the market.

He asked the potter how much he wanted for the dish. The potter, who had spotted a golden coin in Djeha's hand, replied, "Hey! Whatever you're holding is worth as much as the dish."

Djeha gave him the coin, took the dish, and said, "For the love of God, show me how to carry this dish."

"You don't know how to carry it?"

"If I knew, I wouldn't be asking you."

"Give it to me. I will show you how to carry it."

The potter removed the bottom piece, leaving only the sides, which he put over Djeha's head and around his neck. Djeha left on his newly acquired donkey. Back home, his mother asked him, "Son, where is our mule?"

"I traded it for this donkey because it was too tall. I was afraid that one day, I might fall off of it and die. You would have been left alone with nobody to do everything for you."

"And where is the dish that I asked you to buy?"

"It's here, around my neck."

"What! You have taken out the bottom? And how are we supposed to cook with it?"

"I couldn't carry it the way it was, so the potter helped me out. What's more, it only cost me one louis."

"Well then! That's just perfect. Why did you do that? You traded a mule for a donkey and a golden coin for half a piece of pottery! What will people think of us?"

"Mother, the potter told me, 'Red for red, the dish is worth as much as the coin.' So I believed him."

"Dear Lord! Keep the house and do what you want with it. I'm leaving. I'm done with your shenanigans!" his mother said.

"Mother, why would I stay here without you?"

"I'm leaving because you have no common sense!"

Djeha took his donkey and went back to the market. He had covered the donkey completely with golden coins which he had glued to its hide. When he encountered his friends, they asked him how he was doing.

"Very well, thank God. And how have you been?"

"Tell us, did it pay off doing business with us?"

"I continually thank the good Lord. Since I've had your donkey, it has produced nothing but golden louis."

"Bring it here so that we can see for ourselves," the four thieves said.

"It's over there. Come look at it."

One of them went with Djeha. When he was near the donkey, he found it covered in golden coins. He went to his companions and told them, "Let's plead with Djeha. Perhaps he will listen to us and give us back the donkey. It produces nothing but golden coins."

They went to Djeha and said, "If the Lord is your guide, you will fulfill our wish and give us back our donkey. We will give you back your mule and your money."

"I won't accept that deal."

They started begging him.

"If you want it back, add another one hundred *douros*."

"It's a deal."

"In this case, bring me my mule, give me back my one hundred *douros*, add another one hundred *douros* out of your pocket, and you will walk away with your donkey."

Djeha took his mule, climbed up on it and rode home. Before leaving, he gave the robbers these instructions: "Whoever keeps the donkey overnight, should feed it its fill of green grass. They should spread out blankets underneath it. The next day, the blankets will be covered with golden coins."

The thieves left. One of them took the donkey and let it spend the night under his roof. He cut some grass for the donkey and spread out a blanket under its legs. The donkey ate all night and defecated. The following day, when the man checked on it, he found the blankets covered in excrement and picked them up. When one of his companions came and took the donkey, he told him, "My friend, the donkey made me richer. However, you must feed it lots of greens, so that it may eat all night. Put large blankets underneath it and spread them out carefully, so that you won't lose any of the gold coins."

The man left with the donkey. As soon as he got home, he grabbed a sickle, went to his yard, and cut down an entire field of greens to feed the donkey. The next morning, he went to see the donkey and found the blankets drenched in excrement. He folded them up and moved them to the corner.

Now it was the third thief's turn to take the donkey. The donkey did to him what it had done before. The fourth robber came. The donkey repeated what it had done before. Then, the fourth thief went looking for his comrades and said to them, "Seriously? You took all of the golden coins and left me with just the droppings?"

"That wily Djeha has tricked us. Come look at our houses."

They inspected each other's houses and noted that the same had happened there as well.

"Let's go find Djeha and get our revenge."

The Hosts' Pickax

Djeha expected the thieves to arrive on the fourth day. He caught two roosters and two hens, killed them, and cooked them in butter. He added a plate of couscous and buried all the food in his bedroom. He covered everything up with dirt and gave his mother the following instructions, "Mother, today, four men will come here. Watch out. When they arrive, I will keep them company. I will call you and say, 'Bring me the hosts' pickax.' And you will bring it to me."

"Fine."

And indeed, the robbers arrived.

"Good evening, Djeha. How are you?"

"I am doing well, inshallah. And how are you?"

They sat down and started conversing. After a while, Djeha said to his mother, "Bring me the hosts' pickax." She brought it to him. The thieves who were paying close attention had already forgotten their anger. Djeha hit the ground with the pickax and dug up the plate of couscous and the chicken that was cooked in butter.

"Let's eat, friends." They ate.

After the meal, they asked, "Djeha, will you sell us this pickax?"

"I won't sell it to you because my father bequeathed it to me. When I have guests, I don't have to wear myself out. All I have to do is hit the ground with the pickax and, instantly, a plate with couscous and chicken cooked in butter rises from the ground."

"Sell it to us, please!"

"Fine, since we are friends, I will sell it to you."

"May God bless you! We will pay you back. Now, tell us how much you want for it."

"I don't want a lot for it. Just give me one hundred *douros*[6] and it's yours." They handed him the money and left with the pickax. When they got home, one of them took the pickax. That evening, his brother-in-law came over. The man took the pickax and rummaged through the entire house without discovering anything. He put the tool in a corner.

The following day, one of his companions came and said to him, "My friend, give me the pickax."

"Wait, let me get it for you."

He went and got it. His friend took it. When he got home (since he was a sly man and since he hadn't invited any guests yet), he told himself, "I will test this pickax for myself only."

He grabbed the tool, dug in the ground, smashed up his entire house, and found nothing.

"May I become impotent if I tell them what happened before they have smashed up their houses," he muttered to himself, clutching the pickax.

The following day, he went to the village assembly. And that's when the third companion arrived and said to him, "My friend, why don't you go and get me that pickax."

"Wait here. I will get it for you right away."

He went home and fetched the pickax for his friend.

"Here it is."

His friend took it. When he got home, he said to himself, "My family will eat all the food that I will find with this tool. That's better than feeding strangers." He grabbed the pickax and started digging. He smashed up the entire floor of his house and found absolutely nothing. He put the pickax in a corner.

The next day, he went out and met his friend, the fourth thief, who said, "My friend, go and get me that tool." He went home and brought back the pickax. The fourth thief left with the pickax. While he was gone, his mother-in-law had come for a visit.

"Well, the good Lord brought me a guest!" He started searching the ground (in his house) with his pickax. He dug in every corner and found nothing.

"Ah!" he told himself, "My friends have used up all of its magic. I'll go to them right now and take them to court."

When he arrived at his friend's house, the one who had handed him the pickax warned him, "Watch out. The three of you have used up all of its magic, the magic that made the couscous and the chicken appear."

"Come take a look at my house," his friend replied. He went to his house and saw that he had dug everywhere.

"Well, then. Our two friends have tricked us. They used up all the magic. Come on, let's go see them right now."

They left together. When they had arrived at the third robber's house, they told him, "We will sue you because, before passing on the pickax that we bought for five hundred francs, you removed the magic that causes the plate of couscous to rise."

"Come on in and see for yourself," he replied. When they went inside the house, they saw that he had also been digging everywhere.

"Let's go to the first one, everything is his fault," they said. They went to his house and told him, "The four of us bought this pickax for one hundred *douros*. And you are responsible for making the magic that makes the plate of couscous and the chicken rise, disappear!"

"Are you out of your minds or what has gotten into you? Come look at my house and you will see what state it is in."

When they arrived at his house, they noticed that the floors were completely smashed up.

"Why did you not warn us when you noticed that the pickax did not make anything rise to the surface?"

"I didn't tell you because I was afraid that you would call me a liar. And by the way, why is it that the second person who had the pickax did not tell you anything either? Why didn't the third one warn us? Are you telling me that I am the only one you're accusing of eating all the couscous and all the chicken? Let's go pay Djeha a visit and find out what kind of trick he played on us."

"Let's go," they agreed, and off they went.

Djeha's Hare

Djeha was expecting the four thieves on the fourth day. He had three hares. He gave his mother the following instructions, "I'm going to plow the field. You will butcher one of these hares. I will take the other one with me. As for the third one, put it in a corner. When the guys show up, you will tell them that I am working over there. They will come to me. Then, you will prepare lunch with the hare that you butchered."

Djeha left with one of the hares. A while later, the four thieves arrived.

"Where is Djeha?" they asked his mother.

"He is plowing the field over there."

They walked over to him and asked him, "We have come looking for you and you went to work?"

"My friends, if you don't work, you won't eat."

"Why don't you keep us company for a while?"

"In that case, I will have lunch prepared for you."

"Who will you send? Come over here and sit down."

"My messenger is right here," Djeha said, grabbing the hare from under his burnous.

"Go find your mistress and tell her to butcher you and to prepare you for lunch for our guests," he told the rabbit. He let go of the animal, which took off and scurried into the woods.

"What are you doing?"

"Why are you asking me this question?"

"We are confused because you sent home that hare."

"I have another one at home. The two hares were bequeathed to me by my father. When I kill one of them, the other one resuscitates to replace the dead one. I do not have a messenger; that is correct. When friends—like you, for instance—come for a visit and I'm not at home and they come looking for me in the fields—as you did—who could I possibly send home to have lunch prepared for them? If I didn't have a messenger hare, I would have to go home myself and leave you here all alone. Or, if all of us left together, we would arrive at my house at the same time and there would be no lunch waiting for us. This is why I sent my messenger. We will leave together, and the food will be ready for us when we get there."

They stayed for a while longer and left. When they arrived at his house, the hare was cooked and lunch was ready. They were speechless. After they had finished the meal, Djeha showed them the other hare, saying, "Here it is. I told you that when I kill one, the other one resuscitates in its place, didn't I? Here is the messenger I sent earlier. My mother butchered it and prepared it for you to eat. And here's the other one that came back to life in its place. As for this one, the day I will butcher it, the other one will come to life to replace the dead one."

"Djeha, will you sell us this one?"

"My friends, I won't sell it to you because I am childless. This hare is my brother, my son, and my daughter. It acts as my messenger whenever I need one."

"But you will sell it to us because we will pay whatever price you ask for it."

"Honestly, I'd rather not sell you this one. But since you won't take no for an answer, take him."

"Tell us how much you want for it."

"You are my friends. Take it. Let's say it's worth what all the other things we traded in the past were worth."

They gave him one hundred *douros* and left with the hare. They had forgotten all the pranks Djeha had played on them before.

When they got home, one of them told the others, "Today, I will take the hare."

Another one objected, "There are four of us who bought the hare. You will not take it. If you kill it and the other hare does not rise from the dead to replace it, you will have tricked us. Therefore, I will send it home, and my wife will prepare it for dinner. If the other hare resuscitates in its place, then each one of us will take turns taking it. Otherwise, the four of us will eat this one tonight."

"That makes sense," they told each other. They released the hare and ordered it to go home and to tell its mistress to cook it for dinner. Once it had been set free, the hare ran off into the woods. They continued on their way. When they arrived at the house of the person who sent the hare home, they noticed that his wife had not even lit a fire.

"What is going on? Didn't I send someone to tell you to prepare dinner with that hare I sent you?" the husband shouted.

"I haven't seen any hare," his wife answered.

"See, if only one of us had taken the hare home, we would have suspected that person and we would have accused him of eating the hare all by himself and tricking us. However, now it's up to us to decide what to do to the man who has tricked us so many times!" the man said to his friends.

"Let's go to his house and beat him up. Maybe we will even kill him," the three other men replied.

Chapter 6

Religion, Death,
and the Afterlife

The tales in this chapter provide a snapshot of storytelling, vernacular religion, and customs in French Algeria, with all the stereotypes prevalent under the Third Republic (see Reynaud-Paligot 2006; Lorcin [1995] 2004). Most characters depicted in these folktales appear to be Muslims, but in several tales, there are also some Christian and Jewish characters. Historically, non-Muslim minorities lived in Algeria, Morocco, and Tunisia for centuries. At the beginning of the Christian era, Carthage (now Tunisia) and Hippone (the antique name of the Algerian city of Annaba) were strongholds of Christianity. Saint Augustin, one of the fathers of the Roman Church and bishop of Hippone, was a Christian Berber, as was his mother, Saint Monique (Lacoste [1995] 2004, 67). Gradually, Christianity disappeared in the Maghreb, especially in the fifteen century and thereafter, when the last Muslims were driven out of Spain by the Alhambra Decree in 1492 and when the Portuguese and the Spanish launched a series of attacks on the North African shores. With the onset of colonialism, Christianity reappeared with the European colonizers but Muslim conversions to Catholicism were extremely rare (Lacoste and Lacoste [1995] 2004, 67).

Historically speaking, Jewish people were the first non-Berber population that moved to the Maghreb over two thousand years ago and some continue to live there today (Zafrani [1995] 2004, 150). The Arab conquest led to a progressive Islamization of the autochthonous and immigrant populations as well as an Islamization of parts of the Berber Jewish tribes. From the ninth to the eleventh centuries, Jewish culture flourished in the Maghreb, especially around Kairouan, while the advent of the Almohads in the twelfth century forced Jews and Christians into exile unless they were willing to convert to Islam (Alili [1995] 2004, 136). The Jewish minority is as old as the Christian minority: under the Roman Empire, many Berbers had converted to Judaism in opposition to the Emperor Constantine the Great, especially after his conversion to Christianity in Byzantium. The Berber Jews were then joined by the Sephardic Jews that had been expelled from Spain by the Alhambra Decree issued by the Catholic Monarchs of Spain, Isabella I of Castile and Ferdinand II of Aragon. The Jewish quarters in the cities were protected by the authorities. Most of the Jewish minorities left the Maghreb in the wake of rising tensions between Israel and the Arab world. Unlike the Algerian Muslim population, which did not have the right to vote until 1946, the Jewish population had been granted French citizenship by the Crémieux Decree in 1870 and temporarily lost it during the rule of the Vichy government. In 1962, at the end of the Algerian War of Independence, most of the Jews left Algeria for France, along with around one million European settlers, called *pieds-noirs*.

The trickster is omnipresent in the countries bordering the Mediterranean Sea, but depending on the country, he takes on a slightly different name and nationality, and even his religion might change, so that he blends in with the local population and comes across as an ordinary citizen (Nahum 1998, 11). With his Janus personality, Djeha is a malleable folklore character. In some folktales collections he is Muslim, in others Jewish. In the folktales by Tunisian novelist André Nahum (1921–2015), for example, Ch'hâ is Jewish, and in a more recent Sephardic Jewish folktale collection titled *Folktales of Joha, Jewish Trickster* (2003), Joha is also Jewish. Either he has a Christian friend ("The Jewish Festivals," Koén-Sarano 2003, 171), or he regularly argues with his Christian neighbor ("Two Brothers," Koén-Sarano 2003, 166–67). In this collection, Djeha appears to be a Sunni Muslim since he is a student who attends Qur'anic school. As such, he must obey the injunctions of the Qur'an, including the five pillars of Islam (the profession of faith—called *shahada*, praying five times daily, attending the mosque on Fridays, giving alms to the poor, observing Ramadan, and making a pilgrimage to Mecca). He also must refrain from eating pork and drinking alcohol. The tales in this chapter reveal much about vernacular religion, defined as "religion as it is lived: as human beings encounter, understand, interpret, and practice it" (Primiano 1995, 44). The trickster is not an exemplary Muslim. In the tale "Djeha and His Wife," he works on a religious holiday, and in "Djeha and the Christian," he shares a meal with a Christian during Lent and tells him that he is not a rule follower either. Most of the folktale characters in this collection, such as the students and the muezzin, are Muslim. They are seen interacting with Christians and

Jews, often poking fun at each other.[1] While there is no word for humor in classical Arabic, the Qur'an mentions laughter in the sura, "The Star": "It is God who moves to weeping and laughter, who ordains life and death" (53:43, 373). The Qur'an legitimizes and permits relieved laughter and laughter in moderation while condemning vanity and mockery at the expense of other people (see Marzolph 2011, 175–76). The Qur'an states, "Believers, let no man mock another man, who may perhaps be better than himself. Let no woman mock another woman, who may perhaps be better than herself. Do not defame one another, nor call one another by nicknames" ("The Chambers" 49:10, 364).

The Prophet himself condoned laughter, which he considered to be a profoundly human characteristic. "Refresh your hearts periodically, for if they get dull, they become blind" (Rosenthal 1956, 5), the Prophet Muhammad is reported saying. Laughter was welcome and provided a necessary respite from everyday work and constraints.[2] For Djeha, even religion is acceptable to poke fun at. The folktales in this chapter contain jokes at the expense of orthodox Islam ("Djeha and the Sheep's Head") but also Judaism ("The Jew Who Wanted to See God") and Christianity ("Djeha and the Christian"). The trickster mocks believers who practice any of these religions, sometimes with too little or too much zeal. Several folktales mention religiosity, and several recount Djeha's interactions with a Jewish neighbor, who tries to trick Djeha but is outsmarted by him. The portrayal of Djeha's Jewish neighbor as cunning and greedy reflects colonial racial stereotypes that were prevalent under France's Third Republic (1870–1940). According to French folklorist and ethnographer Camille Lacoste-Dujardin, Jews in the Maghreb were victims of xenophobia: "Jewish people were not highly regarded in Kabyle culture, that's the least one can say. They were rejected, [treated] like strangers, even though some Kabyles were believed to be of that same origin" (2005, 200). The same goes for Tunisia, where before the protectorate, Jewish citizens were treated poorly (Nahum 1998, 242).

Similarly, the mention of a female slave in the tale "Djeha Marries a Sultan's Daughter" (chapter 1) reflects a reality in French Algeria, where a highly profitable slave trade continued well after the official abolition of slavery in 1848.[3] Slave characters, both male and female, appear frequently in Arab folktales, for instance in the tale "Sindbad, the Sailor" from *The Arabian Nights*, where the eponymous hero—also a famous trickster figure—recounts how during his seventh and last adventure, he and his sailors were captured by corsairs, how he was sold to a rich Indian merchant, and how he escaped and safely returned to Bagdad.

Djeha's deceiving trickster personality reaches new heights in the tale "Djeha's Knife Kills and Resuscitates." While it is generally God who is believed to have the power to bring the deceased back to life, the trickster pretends to possess a magical knife that lets him exercise supernatural powers. But, of course, he is lying. The Kabyle phrase "Am tjenwit jehha: tnegq theggu" (Like Djeha's knife that kills and resuscitates) is an old Kabyle proverb that refers to seemingly harmless words that are insidiously hurtful (Nacib 2002, 269). In another twentieth-century Berber folktale collected by French linguist and folklorist Jean Delheure, Djeha is endowed with messianic features. He redistributes wealth by giving to the poor things that he took from the rich (Galley and Iraqui Sinaceur 1994, 53). Interestingly, the theme of resuscitation with Djeha's magical knife also appears in the twentieth-century Kabyle folktale "The Green Mountain," where one of the characters utters the magic formula "Jehha's knife kills as it brings back to life" (Nacib 1986, 27). In this case, the young woman who had her throat slashed does indeed come back to life.

In the closing tale, "Djeha's Death," the trickster is finally punished for all of his misdeeds and killed by one of his foes. Cruelly, his murder happens with the complicity of his very best friend, the only human being in whom he had complete trust. As folklorist Henri Basset notes—referring to the deeply entrenched Berber myth—Djeha's death suggests that this leech who managed to live a long and happy life without ever doing any real honest work is not representative of the Berber ideal of industriousness and honesty despite his popularity and general admiration of unscrupulous "bad boy" conduct (1920, 178–79).

Djeha and the Ten Blind People[4]

Djeha was sitting by the river when a group of ten blind people came and said to him, "Take us to the other side of the river. We will give you one franc each."

"It's a deal." He took them across the river one after the other, until he had ferried nine of them across. Djeha went back for the last person and carried him. When he arrived in the middle of the river, the strong current started pulling him away. Djeha let go of the blind person to save his own life. The other blind people started shouting, "Hey there, you're going to let our brother drown!"

"All your shouting is useless. Let's just call it nine francs and forget about the last one."

Djeha and the Christian[5]

One day, Djeha saw a Christian eating meat during the fasting month of Lent. He sat down and shared his meal. "Djeha, Muslims are not allowed to eat animal meat that was butchered by Christians," the Christian said to him.

"I am about as good a Muslim as you are a Christian."

Djeha and the Murder Victim

One day, Djeha discovered the dead body of a man who had been murdered. The killers had left the corpse in his entrance hall. As soon as Djeha saw it, he moved the corpse and threw it down a well.[6] He then went to his father and said, "I have found the body of a man who has been murdered. His corpse had been thrown into our house. I have thrown it down the well."

"No, son. Pull the body out of the well. Perhaps someone will come looking for it in the well and if it were to be found, we would be in trouble. Pull it out of the well now. We will bury the man. It will be better that way." Djeha left, retrieved the corpse, and buried it. He butchered a sheep and threw it down the well.[7]

The parents of the deceased man came looking for their son. When they walked into Djeha's house, he told them, "There is a dead body in this well. Follow me and see if it's him." Djeha climbed down the well, grabbed the sheep's head, called the people, and asked them, "Did your son have horns?" They left confused, muttering, "What an idiot."

The Jew Who Wanted to See God

There was a Jew who said the same prayer to God every day, "Oh God, reveal yourself to me."

He prayed underneath a tree. One day, while he was walking, Djeha overheard him praying like this. The following day, he went to the same place and arrived before the Jew. He climbed up a tree and hid in its foliage. The Jew came and said his usual prayer. Djeha called out to him, "Worshipper, go fetch one hundred dinars [gold coins] and give them to Djeha's wife. Then come back here and you will see me."

The Jew was overjoyed when he heard this. He went home, gathered one hundred gold coins, and gave them to Djeha's wife. He went back to the tree and said,

"Dear Lord, I've done what you told me to do."

Djeha threw him a rope and said, "Grab this rope; you will rise up to me." The Jew took hold of the rope. Djeha pulled him up and when he had reached a certain height, he let go of the rope. The Jew fell and broke his head.

"Dear Lord, you are impossible! You take my money and you also break my head!"

Djeha and Judgment Day[8]

Djeha owned a fat sheep. His friends wanted to trick him so they could eat his sheep. They came to him and said, "Tomorrow is judgment day. Today is our last day in this world. Come with us. We will go to the garden, butcher your sheep, and eat it, because tomorrow, we will die."

Djeha pretended to believe them. He went with them. They butchered the sheep and ate it. When it started getting very hot, they took off their clothes and waded into the river to cool off. Djeha did not go for a swim. Instead, he gathered his friends' clothes and sold them. When his friends got out of the river, they couldn't find their clothes. They waited until Djeha returned and asked him, "Where are our clothes?"

"I have sold them. You told me that tomorrow is judgment day, so I figured that you wouldn't need them anymore."

Djeha's Knife Kills and Resuscitates[9]

The four thieves slept outside. They didn't make it to Djeha's house before nightfall. Assuming that they would not arrive that day, the trickster said to his mother and to his wife, "Tomorrow, someone will come to kill me. I suggest playing another trick to save my life."

"Son, what kind of trick will we play on them?"

"We will fill a bladder with blood and I'll hang it around my wife's neck. When they come here, I will give her an order. She will get mad. I will then stab the bladder with a knife and my wife will fall to the ground. They will be shocked at the sight of blood that will be gushing out of the bladder, and surely they will cry out, 'Alas, Djeha, what have you done!' and they will forget everything that happened in the past."

The following day, they came and called him, "Djeha, come out of your house."

"Who is this?" Djeha asked.

"Your friends."

"May God bless you."

"Come out."

"My dear friends, come inside the house."

"We won't go inside."

"Come on in; you will have lunch and God will look kindly upon you."

They went inside, swearing to each other not to eat anything.

"In God's name, you will eat." Djeha served them lunch and they started eating. Djeha then ordered his wife to bring them some water. She refused to obey. Djeha jumped at her, drew his knife, and stabbed her. She fell to the ground and played dead lying in a pool of blood.

The four individuals told each other, "We just witnessed a murder in his house. This murder happened because of us. What are we going to do now?"

"Eat up and don't worry about anything. I have a knife that kills and brings back to life again," Djeha told them. He walked over to his wife, wiped the knife's blade on her several times, and repeatedly said, "Djeha's knife kills and resuscitates." After a while, she got back up and said to her husband, "Ah! You killed me!"

"I will kill you again and resuscitate you like this to punish you for your rotten mood."

The four companions were stunned.

"Djeha," they said, "sell us this knife."

"I won't sell it to you."

"My dear, please sell it to us. Our wives give us a lot of grief. Whoever gets angry because of his wife will stab her and punish her for her bad disposition. He will then bring her back to life with the magic knife."

"Take it. It's yours."

"How much do you want for it?"

"The same amount as usual."

They gave him one hundred *douros* and went home. When they arrived at the village, one of them took the knife home. In the evening, he called his wife and ordered her to do something. She didn't obey. He jumped at her, stabbed her, and killed her. He went to her and said, "Djeha's knife kills and resuscitates." The wife didn't move.[10] He picked her up and buried her.

The next day, one of his friends took the knife without having been warned that Djeha's knife had killed but not healed his friend's wife. He grabbed the knife and left. Back home, he ordered his wife to bring him some water. She didn't obey. He stabbed her and killed her, just as the first one had done. He carried her outside and buried her.

The next day, the third companion came. The second one had also failed to warn him. He gave his wife an order. When she didn't obey, he jumped to his feet, stabbed her, and killed her. She was as dead as the other wives. He picked her up and buried her. The next day, the fourth man came. His friend did not warn him about anything either. He took the knife and left. When he got home, he ordered his wife to prepare dinner.

"Wait a minute, I am busy right now," she replied.

He got up, stabbed her, and killed her. He carried her outside and buried her. He left right away to meet with his three friends and asked them, "Why is my wife dead? She didn't come back to life. What about your wives?"

"They are all dead."

"In that case, let's go to Djeha's house. This time he is the one who will die and not be resuscitated, because he crossed the line. He even killed our wives! What are we waiting for? Let's go, and God willing, he will die. He will no longer make fun of us. This is the last straw!"

Djeha in the Grave

Djeha guessed that the thieves would come back the following day. He said to his mother, "Mother, some people will visit us tomorrow, and they will kill me. What can we do to save my life?"

"Son, that's for you to figure out."

"Well, in that case, I will dig a grave in the hallway, near the front door. I will hide inside the grave and when they get here, you will hand me the grill with the lighted fire. And I will take the branding iron. When they ask you where I am, you will pretend to cry and tell them that I am dead and that this is my grave."

"Fine," his mother said.

Djeha started digging a grave right away and stepped inside it. He remained there until the evening. When he realized that the people were not coming, he got out. This went on for three days. During the daytime, he stayed inside the grave, at night, he climbed out of it. Finally, on the fourth day, the companions showed up.

"Where is Djeha?" they asked his mother.

She pretended to cry and scratch up her face.

"What is the matter with you? We're asking you where your son is and you're crying! You must be aware of all the crimes he has committed?"

"Alas! My son is dead. That's why I am crying."

"Where is his grave?"

"It's here, by the front door."

They went to it. When they got close to the grave, they noticed a hole.

"Come on," one of them said. "Let's piss on his grave."

Djeha could hear everything they were saying. One of the thieves came closer. The moment he bent over, Djeha touched him with a hot branding iron. The thief jumped back and screamed, "I just got stung!"

Another man came. Djeha did the same thing to him. The men went back home without telling each other that Djeha had branded them with his hot iron. Djeha finally climbed out of his grave.

One day, the thieves met him at the market. They tried to catch him, but he managed to get away. They went to the qadi to complain about him.

"Qadi, this is what Djeha did to us. He even killed our wives."

"What? You claim that Djeha killed your wives?"

"Go get Djeha, and you will see whether we are lying or not."

The judge sent a bailiff to bring back Djeha. As soon as he arrived, he asked the qadi what he wanted from him.

"What have you done to these people?" the judge asked. "They just pressed charges against you."

"Your Honor, these people were my father's slaves. My father is dead. When I was young, they looked down on me and wanted to kill me to take possession of my father's estate."

"Did you just say that these men were your father's slaves and that they want to kill you?"

"Since you won't believe me, take a close look at them. If you don't find the mark of my father's stamp on their buttocks, then you will have proof that I lied and you can have me killed."

The qadi spoke to the four individuals, "This is what he said."

"He is lying."

"Let me take a closer look at all of you. If I find the brand that he was talking about, I will take care of you," the judge said. He examined them and found the brand on their buttocks, as Djeha had told him.

"I sentence you to work for him until he dies."

The crooks left and were forced to work for Djeha until the day he died.

Djeha and the Sheep's Head[11]

The following day, Djeha watched the muezzin climb to the top of the minaret. He followed him, beheaded him, and presented his wife with the head. He told her: "Here is the head of the man who used to wake you up early in the morning."

"If you can get away with murder, I will believe you when you say that you are a sultan."

Djeha left, bought a sheep, and butchered it. He threw the muezzin's head down the well. He hid the sheep's head under a large wooden dish. At around noon, people started looking for the muezzin because he had disappeared. They climbed up the minaret and found his dead, beheaded body.

"Who killed our muezzin?" they wondered.

One of them said, "I saw Djeha climb up here early this morning. Perhaps he is the murderer."

They went to Djeha's house and asked him point blank, "Did you kill our muezzin?"

"I did not. What could he possibly have done to me to make me want to kill him? Why don't you find someone that he didn't get along with; that person must have killed him. I didn't kill him."

"The man who saw you climb up the minaret said you were the murderer. You are lying. We are going to search your house to see if we'll find his head."

"Go ahead and search."

They went inside and started searching. They turned his house upside down and found nothing. One of them noticed a large wooden dish that was flipped over. He picked it up and discovered the sheep's head underneath.

"I just found a sheep's head in what looked like a perfect hiding place. He probably did not kill the muezzin."

They all went home. Djeha got away with murder.

Eagle-Eyed Djeha and His Excellent Marksmanship[12]

With age, Djeha lost his eyesight. He could no longer see as far as he could when he was young. When he was younger, he could spot a partridge or a hare from five hundred feet away, and when he shot an arrow, he never missed the target. But now his hands were shaking, and he couldn't see very well anymore. Having noticed these signs of aging, his neighbors made fun of him every day. To shut them up, he came up with the following plan. He bought a puppy that he named Always Fetch and trained it for hunting. He trained it to fetch anything he showed him. In the morning, he would often hide a dead hare in the mountains. He showed the dog where he hid it, and the two of them went back home. At noontime, he ordered the dog to search. Always Fetch raced up the mountain and, after a while, came back with the hare in its jaw. Finally, the dog was well trained and Djeha waited for the day of the big village feast to prove to everyone that he was still eagle-eyed.

That morning, he had put a dead hare next to a tree, more than five hundred feet away from the village and had shown it to his dog. At noon, he invited his neighbors over for coffee at his house. People started coming from everywhere, and there was a large crowd when, all of a sudden, Djeha got up and shouted, "Dear friends, don't you see a hare over there, by that tree?" They opened their eyes wide, looked carefully, but couldn't see anything.

"You are crazy. How can you possibly spot a hare from this far away?"

"I understand that, given your weak eyesight, you cannot see it, but I can." Turning to his wife he said, "Bring me my bow and arrows. I will show these young people that I still have strong eyes and arms." He took an arrow and shot it as far as the eye can see.

"I killed it!"

Turning to his dog, he said, "Run, Always Fetch, and bring me back the hare; we will eat it tonight." The dog jumped up and raced off. A while later, Always Fetch returned carrying a bloody hare in its mouth.

Everyone was amazed. After Djeha had repeated his trick three or four times, no one made fun of him or doubted his shooting skills anymore. From that day on, the villagers respected him even more than they had in the past.

Djeha's Death

Djeha had a friend. He was the only man in the whole world he trusted. He very often shared meals with him at his house. One day, his friend invited him to go for a walk.

"I'm a busy man, my friend," Djeha said. "However, since you came in person, I'll take a break and come with you. If someone else had come and given me all the earth has to offer, I would not have gone with him. But since it's you, I can't disappoint you."

The two of them left. When they arrived at his friend's house, his friend invited him in.

"My dear friend, this is the women's apartment. It is inappropriate for us to invade their privacy. I'd rather go somewhere else where we will be alone."

What Djeha didn't know was that his friend had dug a pit for him in the women's quarters. He didn't have the slightest idea. When Djeha suggested they go into another room, his friend replied, "Why don't we sit here instead? It is very spacious, the other room is too small for even one person to sit in comfortably."

"Fine, let's do as you wish."

This friend whom he trusted had been promised money if he killed Djeha. His enemies wanted revenge, because Djeha had once harmed them. Djeha's friend invited him into his house. Djeha had no idea that he was about to be killed by his best friend. His friend had covered the pit with a mat, on top of which he had spread out a carpet.[13] When he came in, Djeha noticed a rolled-out carpet. He thought his friend had put the carpet there to honor him. He stepped forward to sit on the carpet and fell into the pit.

The traitor left right away, looking for the people who had promised him money to kill Djeha. He went to them and told them that he had killed Djeha.

"We will come with you to see how you killed him," they said. When they got to his house, they leaned forward and spotted Djeha down at the bottom of the pit.

"Djeha, are you done being stubborn? Now you can't harm us anymore."

"Actually, you did not cause my downfall. It was my friend with whom I often shared meals [food and salt]. He is the one who betrayed me. Sometimes he ate at my house; sometimes I ate at his house. I have never done anything to harm him; he is the one who hurt me."

Turning to Djeha's friend who had captured him, they said, "He is not dead. He might very well climb up. Is he not, after all, the most cunning man who ever lived? He will excavate the walls, dirt will fall to the ground, and he will erode the pit. Then he will come out and kill all of us."

"One of you take this gun and shoot him," Djeha's friend said, handing them a gun.

One of them stepped forward to shoot. Djeha started screaming. Startled by the noise, the man who had fired the shot fell into the pit next to Djeha and died. The gun went off by itself and killed Djeha.[14]

"Djeha has struck again and murdered one of us." Djeha's friend stayed there, while the other man went home. Djeha and the other man lay dead at the bottom of the pit. The betrayer did not collect his money.

Appendix

Notes

Note from the Editor and Translator

1. As Israeli folklorist Matilda Koén-Sarano rightly notes in her collection *Folktales of Joha, Jewish Trickster*, "It is practically impossible to preserve oral folktales in writing. They are formed in the very act of narration, passing from one person to another, from country to country, from generation to generation. Each narrator adapts and alters the elements of a tale around a more or less fixed nucleus, frequently by means of mimicry and according to his or her memory, mood of the moment, character of the audience, and circumstances in which the tale is told. And so every time a tale is told, it emerges differently. With each telling, it is unique and unrepeatable. The real fascination of the folktale resides in this oral quality, which unfortunately is nontransferable. Once set down in writing, a tale loses the theatricality that the narrator's tone of voice and gestures give it. A researcher must therefore decide what written style is most appropriate for a tale. That choice ultimately turns out to be straightforward though not easy, because the author is 'writing' an oral text" (2003, 2).

Introduction: Tracing the Trickster in North African Folktales

1. All translations from the French are mine unless otherwise indicated.

2. The traditional repertoire presents him as a teenager interested in sexuality, while other early anecdotes portray him as a "naïve

philosopher and social critic" (Marzolph 2006, 426). For a contemporary tale in which Djeha impregnates a married woman who then gives birth to a baby girl, see Aceval 2011, 35–36.

3. As Marzolph explains elsewhere, "*adab*-literature by its very definition consists in the organization of useful and entertaining bits of information, which have secured a normative quality by the collective judgment of traditional societal values" (1999, 163).

4. Turkish archaeologists and historians claim that the Hodja, or Hoca, character is inspired by a man born in the town of Sivrihisar, Central Anatolia in 1209, during the Sejkuk Empire. This man died in 1284 in the town of Akşehir, the "White City" (and the ancient town of Philomelion), where he spent most of his lifetime, some 100 kilometers from his birthplace (Maunoury 2011, 8–9). He supposedly studied religion in Aqchahr and Konia. He became a judge and a preacher and was named professor and imam in several cities. He was educated, wise and pious, a cheikh, that is, a master whose wisdom is universally recognized (Schmidt 2005, 150). The Hodja's mausoleum in Akşehir can still be visited today. His original tenth-century tomb has replaced a much older tomb, which, according to legend, was built by the Hodja himself. Pilgrims must have been amused at the site of this strange building made up of one single dome resting on four columns with three of its sides completely open to the outside and only the facade walled and featuring a door locked with a huge padlock. The Hodja's tomb, located at the center of this building was pierced and it is through this tiny hole that he continued to watch the world (Maunoury 2011, 9).

5. Matilda Koén-Sarano, editor of the Sephardic Joha collection *Folktales of Joha, Jewish Trickster* (2003) explains: "Tales of Joha delighted us in our youth, we children of Jews who emigrated from the region of the former Ottoman Empire and from North Africa to Italy, France, Israel, and the Americas. So it is that these tales link us with our parents. We received them in the most direct manner possible: face to face" (3).

6. As Jean Déjeux points out in his study *Djoh'a: héros de la tradition orale arabo-berbère: hier et aujourd'hui*, the two (Djoh'a and Nasreddin Hoca) characters have different historical and geographical origins and should not be conflated or taken for the same character (1978, 15).

7. With regard to the complex development of the trickster character that was fashioned by oral tradition and the *adab* compilations that were published in the second half of the nineteenth century, it is important to point out that there is a correlation between oral tradition and written

sources, which further obfuscates any attempt to clearly delineate the origins and development of the trickster character: "Probably one of the most important steps in the development of a folk narrative research in the twentieth century was the growing awareness of a continuous correlation between oral and written tradition. Oral tradition at the same time both draws from written sources as well as inspires further written production. Seen from the opposite perspective, written tradition exploits the oral while it also serves as a mine of material for reproduction in the oral. Written tradition appears to be the more durable partner of the reciprocally dependent twins, while oral tradition is the more spontaneous one" (Marzolph 1999, 165).

8. Other researchers claim that the trickster was born in the Arab tribe of the Fazâra during the Abbasid Caliphate in the eighth century: the wise men and writer of hadiths Abû I-Ghusn Dujayn ibn Thâbit al-Yarbû'I of Basra was known as Joha and lived at the same time as Abû Ja'far al-Mansûr, Mahdi, and Hârûn ar-Rachîd (Schmidt 2005, 149–50). He is also rumored to have lived in Koufa, southern Iraq, in the eighth century (Mouliéras and Déjeux 1989, 11). Moroccans claim that the "real" Djoh'a is from Fez, where a street is named after him (Déjeux 1987, 16). Algerian folklorists claim that he was inhumed in Algeria, where people to this day pilgrimage to his tomb and worship him as a saint (Zoubeida 2013, 31). Tunisia also lays claim to the trickster: Ch'hâ's tomb is said to be located in a cemetery near Bab el Khadra in Tunis, in the vicinity of another mythical tomb, that of the legendary last of the Moorish tribe of the Abencerrages, who held a high position in the kingdom of Granada and whose life was recounted by François-René de Chateaubriand (Benattar 1923, 185). Whether or not this legendary character really existed is not all that important to determine.

9. On humor in Islam, see Marzolph 1992, 2009, 2011.

10. Shahriyar had his first wife killed because she had made him a cuckold. To avoid suffering the same fate, Shahrazad tells her husband, King Shahriyar, stories every night until dawn. She promises the king to tell an even more wonderful story the following night if her life is spared. Mesmerized by Shahrazad's tales, the king eventually decides to spare her life. He decides that she must love him since she bore him three children during those one thousand and one nights.

11. Incidentally, several jocular Djeha tales appear in select manuscripts of *The Arabian Nights*, for instance in the "Barber's Tale of His Fifth Brother" of the 162nd night (see Marzolph 2005, 319). However,

occurrences of such jocular tales are rare: "Juḥā does not figure promi-
nently in the *Arabian Nights*, if at all, and there is good reason why his
mention in the Madrid manuscript remains a singular phenomenon"
(Marzolph 2005, 322).

12. A Palestinian trickster collection titled *Tales of Juha* underlines
the multidimensional and ambivalent dimension of the character that
appears in many opposite roles: "Shepherd, judge, merchant, scholar,
saint, thief. . . . More generally, he appears as a wealthy man or pauper,
generous man or miser, intelligent man or simpleton, bachelor or married man" (Jayyusi 2007, 6).

13. Notable collections are Taos Marguerite Amrouche's folktale
collection *Le Grain magique: contes, poèmes et proverbes berbères de
Kabylie* (1966; *The Magic Seed: Tales, Poems and Berber Proverbs from
Kabylia*), Mouloud Feraoun's collection *Les Poèmes de Si Mohand* (1960;
The Poems of Si Mohand), Malek Ouary's collection of poems and songs
Poèmes et chants de Kabylie (1974; *Poems and Songs from Kabylia*), and
Mouloud Mammeri's Berber folktale collection *Machao! Contes berbères
de Kabylie* (1980; *Machao! Berber Tales from Kabylia*), to name but a few.

14. For North African Francophone writers in general, the dissemination of their work is important. The use of French is perceived as
liberating because it allows them to transgress taboos and write about
things (such as alcohol, eroticism, prostitution, and homosexuality) that
couldn't be addressed in classical Arabic, the language of the Qur'an
(Ben Jelloun [1995] 2004, 98).

15. Tlemcen is a town in northwestern Algeria located near the
Moroccan border. It is also the birthplace of Algerian novelist Moham-
med Dib (1920–2003), who incidentally also devoted two texts to Djeha:
"Zizi Kadda" and the short story "Le Companion" (see Déjeux 1976).

16. Burke might find Alan Dundes's *Folklore Matters* (1989)
enlightening.

17. Also see Albert Wesselski's *Der Hodscha Nasreddin* (1911), a two-
volume collection that features Turkish, Arabic, Berber, Sicilian, Cal-
abrian, Croatian, Serbian, and Greek trickster tales.

18. As Marzolph remarks, "Similar to the expansion of the narrative
repertoire attributed to him, the depiction of Juha's character has also
undergone considerable development. The traditional repertoire presents him mostly as an adolescent with a certain preference for sexual,
scatological, and otherwise 'obscene' matters. Even so, the early anecdotes already imply some of the more charming traits of the character,

such as when he buries his money in the desert and remembers the position of a specific cloud so as to locate the place later" (2006, 426). Similarly, Muhammad Zarrouki describes the poetic inclination of the trickster as follows: "Once somebody asked him what happened to the moon after passing its last quarter. 'What happens to it? What did you learn in the school? You must know that one breaks it into pieces in order to make the stars'" (1951, 19).

19. In the tale "Djoha and the Pacha," the trickster describes himself as the village idiot, who, when subject to spells of dementia in late afternoons, will say the exact opposite of what he thinks (Ben Danou 1971, 39–41).

20. Interestingly, legend connects the Turkish Nasreddin Hoca to the "life of a great Muslim mystic Mansur al Hallaj, who was executed in the tenth century AD for his unorthodox behavior" (Başgöz and Boratav 1998, 7).

21. Incarnation of a protective spirit who guarded people and their homes; in Kabylia, places inhabited by guardians, incarnations of spirits that protect people and their homes: trees, woods, springs, and rocks.

22. According to Marzolph, early Arabic sources (primarily but not exclusively Shiite Muslim sources from Iraq and Azerbaijan, among others) from the ninth and tenth centuries depict Buhlūl (i.e., *buhloul*), who died in 190/805, as a wise madman who at some point lost his marbles and dropped out of society (1991, 275). He was an educated person who was extremely knowledgeable, having memorized the Qur'an, hadith, and poetry as a younger teenager. For more information on this pseudohistorical character, see Marzolph's study *Der Weise Narr Buhlūl* (1983) and Dols (1992).

23. In that respect, Djeha is exactly like the Turkish Nasreddin Hoca character, who is equally complex and unpredictable: "cunning and clever, but sometimes stupid; sometimes intelligent, sometimes a fool; a folk philosopher and a social critic, but as well a trickster; a national hero and numbskull; or all of the above at once" (Başgöz and Boratav 1998, 4). That said, Nasreddin is often portrayed as a figure of authority, while Djeha is more of an underdog. In the foreword of his French translation of Turkish trickster tales, titled *Les Plaisanteries de Nasr-Eddin Hodja*, French Orientalist Jean-Adolphe Decourdemanche writes that the term "Hodja" designates an ecclesiastical figure (an *abbé*), a judge, or a schoolmaster (1876).

24. Multiple reincarnations and facets of the Djeha character have resurfaced in recent Algerian Francophone texts, including in the short

story "The Companion" in the collection *Au Café* (1955; *At the Café*) by
Mohammed Dib, the play *Mohamed, prends ta valise* (1975; *Mohamed,
Grab Your Suitcase*) by Kateb Yacine, and the novel *L'Insolation* (1972) by
Rachid Boudjedra (see Déjeux 1976 and 1978). The character of the wise
madman also resurfaces in Moroccan writer Tahar Ben Jelloun's novel
Moha le fou, Moha le sage (1978, see Jones 2012a) and in the Tunisian
film *Goha* (1958, dir. Jacques Baratier) with Omar Sharif in the role of
the trickster.

25. Variants of these tales can be found in Denys Johnson-Davies's
board book *Goha, the Wise Fool* (2005), which focuses on the Egyptian
folk hero variant and features illustrations of beautiful tapestries.

Chapter 1. Family and Kinship

1. Folklorist Youssef Nacib notes the existence of "sporadic cases of
polygamy, traditionally in the Djurdjura mountains" (2002, 63). Though
Djeha is not a polygamist in Mouliéras's Berber folktale collection, he
occasionally is a polygamist elsewhere, for example in "The Two Wives"
("Les Deux Épouses"; see Muzi 2009, 197; also see Zarrouki 1951, 19). In
this Algerian tale, Djeha tells his pretty second wife that he wouldn't
have to save her from drowning since she knows how to swim, implying
that he would let the ugly first wife drown because he loves her less. In
a funny Turkish Nasreddin Hoca variant of the same tale, the trickster
also has to please his two competing wives. Asked which one he would
save from drowning because he loved her more, he asks the older wife,
"You know how to swim, don't you, dear wife?" (see Başgöz and Boratav
1998, 116). In a Palestinian tale, the trickster has two wives to whom
he secretly gives the same necklace. When asked by one of his wives
who he loves best, he replies the one who he gave a necklace to as a
present. This is how the tale ends: "And so they were both happy and
contented, each believing she was the favored one" (Jayyusi 2007, 21–22).
For a Nasreddin Hoca variant of this tale dealing with jealous cowives,
see Muzi 2009, 198–99.

2. Muslim voluntary fast day observed on the tenth day of Muharram
(first month of the Islamic year); Shiite Muslims commemorate the
death of Husayn during the Battle of Karbala.

3. Sacrificial feast during which Muslims butcher a sheep to commemorate the sacrifice of Abraham.

4. The family of the Turkish Nasreddin Hoca trickster is also presented as a nuclear family (see Başgöz and Boratav 1998, 20).

5. For more information on the gendered dichotomy of space, see Bourdieu's essay "The Sense of Honour" (1979, 124).

6. In a wider sense, the term refers to rules that concern each and every action of a Muslim person.

7. On women's wiles (already mentioned in the Qur'an), see Keller 2018.

8. The treasure motif appears often in the early anecdotes that "imply some of the more charming traits of the character, such as when he buries his money in the desert and remembers the position of a specific cloud so as to locate the place later" (Marzolph 2006, 426).

9. Ch'ha's nail is equivalent to the English expression "pain in the butt." I wish to thank the second anonymous reviewer for pointing this out to me.

10. Considered a symbol of honor and virility, a burnous is a hooded cloak worn by men for protection from the cold, the wind and/or sand. It is also a beautifully embroidered coat featuring upside down triangles that are sown with blue or white silk threads. See Nacib (1981, 33) for a detailed description of a traditional burnous.

11. For a short variant from the Algerian city Ouargla, see Delheure (quoted in Déjeux 1978, 79). The folktale "Joha's Nail" is also popular in Sephardic Jewish, Judeo-Spanish (also called Ladino) tradition. In this variant, Joha insists on keeping ownership of the nail in the wall because it is a souvenir from his deceased father. He later hangs a dead cat from it (see Koén-Sarano 2003, 61–62). For a shorter Palestinian variant of this tale, see Jayyusi 2007, 67. For a Nasreddin Hoca variant, see Muzi 2009, 135–38.

12. One *douro* was worth five francs. In reality, traditional precapitalist Berber economies were barter economies based on the exchange of goods against other goods (see Bourdieu 1977, 22–27).

13. Shoes were objects loaded with symbolism in traditional Berber culture. Women were under no circumstances allowed to wear men's shoes, because it was believed that doing so would make them sterile and it would therefore be impossible for them to get married or for widows to remarry. Only men were allowed to wear cow leather shoes purchased at the market. Wearing shoes allowed men to symbolically take possession of their lands, something women were precluded from doing (see Servier 1962, 124–25). In a Sephardic Jewish variant of this tale, titled "The Paper Shoes," Joha is upset because his mother has

a lover. She asks her son to buy her a pair of shoes for the festival of Rosh Hashana. When she asks him why he bought her a pair of paper shoes, the trickster replies, "Mama . . . if you put them on only on Rosh Hashana night to meet your boyfriend, they will last a very long time!" (Koén-Sarano 2003, 33).

14. Berber onomatopoeic hoot of owl.

15. (Male) meeting, assembly. For more information on this exclusively male gathering place, see Nacib 1981, 96.

16. A variant of this folktale, titled "A Very Strange Tomb," is documented in Sephardic Jewish tradition (see Koén-Sarano 2003, 272).

17. In another Algerian variant, titled "Djoha et les mouches" ("Djeha and the Flies"), the trickster "sells" a cow that he had butchered to a huge fly (see Ben Danou 1971, 19–23). When he goes back to the market to demand payment, the cow has been devoured by stray dogs and the fly is nowhere to be found.

18. The popular motif "Making the princess laugh or smile" appears in the popular folktale "Jack and the Beanstalk." Jack manages to make the princess smile with the help of his magic beanstalk and eventually marries her after setting her emotionally free (see Bettelheim 1976, 185–86). It is also at the center of the tale "The Princess Who Never Smiled" by Alexander Afanasyev and the "The Golden Goose" by the Brothers Grimm.

19. For the continuation of this tale, see the tale "Djeha and the Sheep's Head" in chapter 6.

20. For a Sephardic Jewish variant of this tale, see "The Lucky Shirt" (Koén-Sarano 2003, 212). In a Nasreddin Hoca variant of this tale, the trickster shoots an arrow at his own caftan and is relieved that he wasn't wearing it at the time: "Thank God I was not in the caftan. Otherwise, I would have killed myself" (Başgöz and Boratav 1998, 136–37).

Chapter 2. Animal Tales

1. Numerous Nasreddin Hoca tales feature a donkey. In one tale, the trickster's donkey revolts and goes to court because he is fed up with carrying heavy loads and being beaten (see Başgöz and Boratav 1998, 154–55).

2. Other trickster tale collections also highlight the importance of the donkey (see Belamri 1991; Finbert 1929; Ben Danou 1971; Nahum 1998, 2000).

3. In 1845, French orientalist, journalist, painter, writer, and Parnassian poet Théophile Gautier (1871–1872) joined General Bugeaud's Kabylia expedition for a three-month journey and visited Algiers, Blida, Constantine, and Oran (Richardson 1958, 76). In his travelogue *Far from Paris*, Gautier lamented the commodification of donkeys in North Africa and wrote about animal abuse: "To be a carriage horse in Paris, that's a sad fate; but to be a donkey in Algiers, what a deplorable situation! What a crime are these poor animals atoning for . . . ? They are never given anything to eat or drink: they live by the hazard of the garbage they find, wisps of straw and bits of wickerwork they tear off in passing" (1865, 42). Ironically, it did not occur to him that the French Republic exploited North Africa as a commodity as well (see Jones 2017).

4. There is indeed an identical Nasreddin Hoca folktale (see Başgöz and Boratav 1998, 29–30).

5. For further explanation of why dogs were not to be allowed inside a house, see the religious legend "The Angels and the Dog" ("Les Anges et le chien"), Basset 1927, 3, no. 12.

6. For Sephardic Jewish variants of this tale, see "If God Wills It!" (Koén-Sarano 2003, 193–94) and "Incorrigible" (Koén-Sarano 2003, 201).

7. In a Nasreddin Hoca variant of this tale, the Hoca ends up serving his guest bread and water instead of a cooked hare dish (see Başgöz and Boratav 1998, 133).

8. See "Le Corbeau" ("The Raven," Muzi 2009, 90) for an identical Nasreddin Hoca variant.

9. For an identical Nasreddin Hoca variant of this tale, see "Words" ("Paroles," Muzi 2009, 84).

10. In a Nasreddin Hoca variant of this tale, the Hoca talks to his donkey and tells his neighbor: "My donkey doesn't agree to this. He says, 'Don't give me to a foreigner. They would hit my ears, and they also curse your wife'" (Başgöz and Boratav 1998, 134–35). For a Djeha variant of this tale, see "Le Refus de l'âne" ("The Donkey's Refusal," Muzi 2009, 83).

11. This tale is a sequel to the tale "Djeha and the Goat Hide" (chapter 1). A variant of this folktale, titled "Donkey on a Diet," exists in Sephardic Jewish tradition. Joha sells a donkey that supposedly defecates Napoleonic coins overnight when fed a proper diet of barley and water. Unfortunately, instead of making its new owner rich, the donkey dies overnight (see Koén-Sarano 2003, 75–76). In a much shorter variant from Ouargla, titled "The She-Ass That Defecates Money" ("L'Ânesse

qui expulse de l'argent"), the trickster is summoned to appear in court after his she-ass fails to produce money (see Delheure, quoted in Déjeux 1978, 81–82).

12. The members of this religious and mystical brotherhood engaged in rituals involving dancing, music, and animal sacrifices.

Chapter 3. Faces, Places, or Daily Life in the Village

1. Djeha might be poor, but he is carefree and smart, and he excels at making people laugh. His rebellious and irreverent laughter-provoking attitude make him (much like Rabelais's characters Gargantua and Pantagruel) a free character. As Russian literary theorist and medievalist Mikhail Bakhtin states in *Rabelais and His World*, "Next to the universality of medieval laughter we must stress another striking peculiarity: its indissoluble and essential relation to freedom" (1984, 89). Given his poverty, laughter and self-mockery are indispensable survival tools.

2. On theories of laughter and humor, also see Schaeffer 1981; Chabanne 2002; and Scherb 2003.

3. Traditional Berber law was written in judicial books called *qanoun*, which specified punishments for various offenses, including murder, infliction of injuries and wounds, violent disputes, disrespect of women, and theft (of fruit and vegetables) from gardens (see Basset 1920, 92).

4. For an identical Palestinian variant of this tale, see Jayyusi 2007, 115. For identical Nasreddin Hoca variants of this tale, see Başgöz and Boratav (1998, 43) and Muzi (2009, 133).

5. For a Nasreddin Hoca variant of this tale, see "The Rooster and the Hens" ("Le Coq et les poules," Muzi 2009, 51–53).

6. Judges did not enjoy the best reputation in French Algeria. In Alphonse Daudet's best-selling novel *Tartarin of Tarascon* (first published in French in 1872), the narrator accuses them of corruption, laziness, gluttony, and debauchery:

> It is the justice of the conscienceless, bespectacled cadis [*sic*] under the palm-tree, Mawworms of the Koran and Law, who dream languidly of promotion and sell their decrees, as Esau did his birthright, for a dish of lentils or sweetened kouskous [*sic*]. *Drunken and libertine cadis are they, formerly servants to*

some General Yusuf or the like, who get intoxicated on champagne,
along with laundresses from Port Mahon, and fatten on roast mut-
ton, whilst before their tents the whole tribe waste away with hun-
ger, and fight with the harriers for the bones of the lordly feast....
This is what Tartarin might have seen had he given himself the
trouble; but wrapped up entirely in his leonine-hunger, the son
of Tarascon went straight on, looking to neither right nor left, his
eyes steadfastly fixed on the imaginary monsters which never
really appeared. (Daudet and Rhys 1921, 75; emphasis mine)

For a Palestinian variant, see Jayyusi 2007, 107, and for a near-identi-
cal Nasreddin Hoca variant of this tale, see Başgöz and Boratav 1998, 33.

7. For a Sephardic Jewish variant of this tale, see "If They Give You,
Take . . ." (Koén-Sarano 2003, 195). In this folktale, Joha is Jewish and
has a rich upstairs neighbor; also see Jayyusi 2007, 68–70, for another
variant of this tale that is about the trickster's quarrel with a neighbor.
Yet another French variant of this tale, "Djoha et l'avare" ("Djeha and
the Penny Pincher"), appears in *Aventures de Djoha* (see Ben Danou
1971, 29–34). There is a Nasreddin Hoca variant of this tale in which
the neighbor is also Jewish (see Başgöz and Boratav 1998, 37–38). In yet
another variant, "Le Rêve de Nasreddine Hodja" ("Nasreddin Hodja's
Dream"), the trickster dreams that a stranger he meets on the street
offers him nine golden coins. The trickster asks for ten coins to round
up the sum but ends up taking the nine coins (see Muzi 2009, 116).

8. Chief of the Berber tribal communities of the Atlas region.

9. For a Sephardic Jewish variant of this tale, see "Dangerous Hair-
cut" (Koén-Sarano 2003, 179–80). In a Nasreddin Hoca variant of this
tale, the Hoca wants to get two haircuts for the price of one because he
is bald (see Başgöz and Boratav 1998, 127).

10. For a Sephardic Jewish variant of this tale, see "An Eye for an Eye"
(Koén-Sarano 2003, 180). In a Nasreddin Hoca variant of this tale, the
Hoca is replacing the tiles on his roof (see Başgöz and Boratav 1998, 134).

Chapter 4. Foodways

1. The hospitality motif also appears in the folktale "Ali Baba and the
Forty Thieves" in *The Arabian Nights*, where Ali Baba invites—unbeknownst

to him—into his home the leader of the thieves—disguised as an oil merchant—and his thirty-seven mules (each mule charged with oil vases containing one thief).

2. In a Sephardic Jewish variant of this tale, titled "The Chicken," a neighbor brings Joha a chicken, which the trickster cooks every day for various guests until there is nothing left but a pot of a smelly, watery soup. The trickster tells his dismayed guests, "Look, this is the soup of the soup from the bones of the chicken that the friend of the neighbors of your friends brought me" (Koén-Saran 2003, 255).

3. In an identical Algerian variant of this tale, he recites the Fatiha over the poultry (see untitled tale in the chapter titled "Djoha the Parasite," Ben Danou 1971, 156–57).

4. For an identical Djeha variant of this folktale, titled "La Viande ou le chat" ("The Meat or the Cat"), see Muzi 2009, 200–201.

5. For an identical Nasreddin Hoca variant of this tale, see Muzi 2009, 172.

6. For a Djeha variant of this tale, "How to Get Invited" ("Savoir s'inviter"), see Muzi 2009, 161.

7. For a Djeha variant of this tale that features sheep instead of bread, see Muzi 2009, 1986.

8. For Djeha variants of this tale, see Ben Danou 1971, 73–75 and Muzi 2009, 126–27. Inea Bushnaq's book *Arab Folktales* contains an identical Syrian variant titled "Djuha Borrows a Pot" (1986, 254–55), attesting to the wide dissemination of this tale, which also exists in Sephardic Jewish tradition ("Djeha and the Washtub," Koén-Sarano 2003, 158). In a Palestinian variant of this tale, Juha explains to his neighbor that his pot died in childbirth (see Jayyusi 2007, 67–68). In a Nasreddin Hoca variant of this tale, the trickster says, "My dear neighbor, you believed that a cauldron gave birth, didn't you?" (see Başgöz and Boratav 1998, 58).

9. For an Algerian variant of this tale, see "Djoha and His Master" ("Djoha et son maître," Ben Danou 1971, 25–27). For a Sephardic Jewish variant of this tale, see the folktale "Spicy Dish" (Koén-Sarano 2003, 248).

10. In a Palestinian variant of this tale, the trickster sends his son to the marketplace to buy him a grilled sheep's head and his son eats it all and explains to his father that he bought it that way (see Jayyusi 2007, 95–96).

Chapter 5. The Intricacies of Hospitality:
Beware of Friends and Foes!

1. Nahum adds, "It is during the *seder*, referred to as the Last Supper, that Jesus had the problems we know about with Judas and the Roman soldiers" (1998, 36).

2. In Alphonse Daudet's 1872 novel *Tartarin de Tarascon*, the narrator derides the sacred concept of hospitality, which, he claims, does not come free of charge: "Everywhere, too, Tartarin was given splendrous [*sic*] galas, *diffas*, and *fantasias*, which being interpreted, means feasts and circuses. In his honor whole *goums* [unit of native soldiers under French officers in North Africa] blazed away powder, and floated their burnouses in the sun. *When the powder was burned, the agha* [man of authority or religious leader] *would come and hand in his bill. This is what is called Arab hospitality*" (Daudet and Rhys 1921, 75–76; emphasis mine). Like many of his fellow writers (e.g., orientalists Théophile Gautier, Jean Lorrain, Pierre Loti, Guy de Maupassant, and Eugène Fromentin, who also travelled to North Africa), Alphonse Daudet spent four months in Algeria (from December 1862 to March 1863) and visited Algiers, Blida, Chiffa, and Orléansville. While Pierre Loti, who traveled to Morocco in 1889, very much looked forward to sharing gargantuan diffas ("There are something like twenty-two courses. . . . There are quarters of sheep, pyramids of chickens, mountains of fish, couscous as for an ogre's feast," 197–98), Maupassant, who traveled to Algeria in 1881, grew weary of the daily diet of lamb and couscous and was ecstatic when he was finally able to eat fresh fruit instead: "No roast mutton for breakfast! What joy! No kouskous [*sic*]! Grapes, figs, apricots, instead! This fruit was not very ripe, but we ate it just the same (1903, 75). Overall, the culinary traditions of North African tribes were quite disorienting for the French travelers (see Jones 2017).

3. In a short Nasreddin Hoca variant of this tale, the Hoca also follows the burglar to move in with him (see Başgöz and Boratav 1998, 130). For another Nasreddin Hoca variant in which the trickster threatens to move in with the thief, see Muzi 2009, 128–29.

4. In a Nasreddin Hoca variant of this tale, the Hoca attends a banquet to which he was not invited and gobbles down all the food (see Başgöz and Boratav 1998, 123).

5. In a variant from Ouargla titled "Djoh'a and His Friends" ("Djoh'a et ses amis"), the trickster invites his friends over for tea and sells their

shoes in order to buy tea, peanuts, and sugar; see Delheure (quoted in Déjeux 1978, 87–88).

6. The equivalent of five hundred francs.

Chapter 6. Religion, Death, and the Afterlife

1. For example, in a Nasreddin Hoca tale, a priest asks the Hoca how the Prophet Muhammad ascended into heaven. The Hoca says, "By climbing the stairs that were prepared for Jesus Christ" (Başgöz and Boratav 1998, 152).

2. See Mir (1991) for specific examples revolving around the Prophet Moses that showcase the use of humor in the Qur'an, which serves to reinforce theological teachings.

3. On the trade of Sudanese slaves in the Maghreb, see Dermenghem 1954, 244–97.

4. For an identical Nasreddin Hoca variant, see Muzi 2009, 232. In a Tunisian variant of this tale, titled "Les Petits Métiers de Ch'hâ" ("Ch'hâ's Odd Jobs"), Djeha carries his nicely dressed relatives that have just attended a wedding on his back across the river in exchange for nine *rials*. After carrying nine across, he gets too tired to help the last one and tells them to keep one *rial* (see Nahum 1998, 164–66). Interestingly, there is an identical Nasreddin Hoca tale (see Başgöz and Boratav 1998, 19).

5. For an identical Djeha variant, titled "Complicité" ("Complicity"), see Muzi 2009, 216. In a Sephardic Jewish variant of this tale, titled "Fasting the Joha Way," the trickster eats on Yom Kippur, and after the holiday gorges himself with his family. His wife is very upset with him: "What a strange fellow you are, Joha! You don't fast, and you sit and eat like the rest of us, as if you had fasted. Shame on you!" "Why are you so upset? I couldn't keep the fast. . . . But at least I am breaking it!" (Koén-Sarano 2003, 253).

6. "Disposing of the Corpse" (number 1536 in Uther's index) is a popular motif: "The motif of having to get rid of a corpse appears in a series of different narratives. It has different results depending on its situation in the tale" (Uther 2004, vol. 2, 269).

7. This tale is a variant of tale type 1381C, "The Buried Sheep's Head" (Uther 2004, vol. 2, 188), where a man kills a sheep but tells his wife that he killed a man.

8. A variant of this tale, "The End of the World," is documented in the Sephardic Jewish tradition (Koén-Sarano 2003, 165–66). Joha's friends talk him into slaughtering his sheep to have one last nice meal. While roasting his beloved sheep, Joha realizes that he was tricked. While his friends are swimming in the river naked, he collects their clothes and shoes and burns them.

9. This tale, the sequel to the tale "Djeha's Hare" (chapter 5), subverts a type of tale characterized as "Religious Tales: God Rewards and Punishes." Interestingly, legend has it that the Turkish Nasreddin Hoca was also a great miracle worker, said to be able to revive dead animals (Başgöz and Boratav 1998, 7).

10. This tale is a variant of tale type 753A "Unsuccessful Resuscitation": "Christ (St. Peter, angel) resuscitates a dead princess (girl). A companion tries to do the same, fails, and is warned against trying again (is condemned and rescued by Christ)" (Uther 2004, vol. 1, 408).

11. In a Tunisian Jewish variant of this tale, "The Day It Was Raining Sausages and Fava Beans," Djeha beheads the muezzin and throws his head in his well, all because his mother complains that the muezzin wakes her up too early, forcing her to get up early in the freezing morning to go out and work (Nahum 1998, 122–24). To cover up this heinous crime, the mother replaces the head with a ram's head and cooks, as the title indicates, a luscious, "miraculous" meal to distract the villagers' attention from Djeha's murder, hoping that her son won't be identified as the murderer and put on trial. In an Algerian variant from Ouargla titled "Djoha and the Muezzin" ("Djoh'a et le muezzin"), Djoh'a kills the muezzin because he is annoyed that he cannot sleep in (see Delheure, quoted in Déjeux 1978, 88–89).

12. For a Sephardic Jewish variant of this tale, see "The Strength of Age" (Koén-Sarano 2003, 186–87).

13. This tale can be linked to tale type 1086, "Jumping into the Ground," which also features a pit that has been covered up to trick an opponent, in this instance to kill Djeha: "An ogre (giant, devil) and a man (boy, gypsy) have a contest to see who can jump deeper into the ground (can get the earth's bowels out). The man wins because he has dug a pit beforehand and covered it with boughs or a mat (buried fish guts in the ground)" (Uther 2004, vol. 2, 32).

14. This is a variant of tale type 1228, "Firing the Gun," in which a gun is either fired or goes off and kills people (Uther 2004, vol. 2, 81).

References

Primary Source

Mouliéras, Auguste, ed. 1892. *Les Fourberies de Si Djeh'a*. Paris: Ernest Leroux. https://books.google.com/books/about/Les_fourberies_de_Si_Djeh_a.html?id=uHEBe3SqfWoC.

Selected Djeha and Nasreddin Hoca Tales

Aceval, Nora. 2013. *La Femme de Djha, plus rusée que le diable!* Neuilly: Al Manar.

Ben Danou, Edmond. 1971. *Aventures de Djoha*. Paris: Éditions G. P.

Bushnaq, Inea, ed. 1986. *Arab Folktales*. New York: Pantheon Books.

Decourdemanche, Jean-Adolphe, ed. 1876. *Les Plaisanteries de Nasr-Eddin Hodja*. Paris: Éditions Ernest Leroux. https://gallica.bnf.fr/ark:/12148/bpt6k15034154/f11.item.

Delais, Jeanne. 1986. *Les Mille et un rires de Dj'ha*. Paris: L'Harmattan.

Delheure, Jean, trans. "Facéties de Djoh'a d'Ouargla." In *Djoh'a: héros de la tradition orale arabo-berbère: hier et aujourd'hui*, edited by Jean Déjeux, 67–90. Sherbrooke: Naaman.

Farrāj, ʿAbd al-Sattār Aḥmad, ed. 1980. *Akhbār Juḥā*. Cairo: Maktabat Miṣr.

Finbert, Elian-J., ed. 1929. *Les Contes de Goha: contes populaires égyptiens*. Paris: Victor Attinger.

Frobenius, Leo Viktor, ed. 1921–1922. *Volksmärchen der Kabylen*. Jena: Diedrichs.

Jayyusi, Salma, ed. 2007. *Tales of Juha: Classic Arab Folk Humor*, translated by Matthew Sorensen. Northampton: Interlink Books.

Koén-Sarano, Matilda, ed. 2003. *Folktales of Joha, Jewish Trickster*, translated by David Herman. Philadelphia: The Jewish Publication Society.

Leroy, Didier, ed. 1988. *Les Aventures de l'incomparable Mollâ Nasroddine Bouffon de la Perse*. Paris: Souffles.

Maunoury, Jean-Louis, ed. 1994. *Hautes sottises de Nasr Eddin Hodja*. Paris: Phébus.

Maunoury, Jean-Louis, ed. 2002a. *Les Aventures de l'incomparable Nasr Eddin Hodja*. Paris: Phébus.

Maunoury, Jean-Louis, ed. 2002b. *Nasr Eddin Hodja: la soupe au Piment et autres sublimes idioties*. Paris: Phébus.

Maunoury, Jean-Louis, ed. 2002c. *Sublimes paroles et idioties de Nasr Eddin Hodja*. Paris: Phébus.

Maunoury, Jean-Louis, ed. 2006. *Absurdités et paradoxes de Nasr Eddin Hodja*. Paris: Phébus.

Maunoury, Jean-Louis, ed. 2011. *La Sagesse extravagante de Nasr Eddin*. Paris: Albin Michel.

Maunoury, Jean-Louis, ed. 2017. *Les Sages inépties de Nasr Eddin Hodja*. Paris: Albin Michel.

Mouliéras, Auguste and Jean Déjeux, eds. 1987. *Les Fourberies de Si Djeh'a*. Paris: La Boîte à Documents.

Muzi, Jean, ed. 2009. *Contes des sages et facétieux Djeha et Nasreddine Hodja*. Paris: Seuil.

Nahum, André, ed. 1978. *Histoires de Ch'ha*. Paris: Piranhas.

Nahum, André, ed. 1986. *Histoires de Ch'ha ou Jehâ ou Johâ ou Goha, le plus fou d'entre les fous, le plus sage, le plus rusé, le plus naïf, le plus sot et le plus intelligent, l'unique, le seul menteur qui ne dit que la vérité*. Paris: Bibliophane.

Nahum, André, ed. 1998. *Humour et sagesse judéo-arabes: histoires de Ch'hâ, proverbes, etc*. Paris: Desclée de Brouwer.

Nahum, André, ed. 2000. *Tunis-la juive-raconte*. Paris: Desclée de Brouwer.

Najjār, Muhammad Rajab. 1978. *Juha al-'Arabi*. Kuwait: Alam al-Marifa.

Wesselski, Albert, ed. 1911. *Der Hodscha Nasreddin: türkische, arabische, berberische, maltesische, sizilianische, kalabrische, kroatische,*

serbische und griechische Märlein und Schwänke. Weimar:
Alexander Duncker Verlag. Vol. 1: https://www.gutenberg.org/files
/54690/54690-h/54690-h.htm; Vol. 2: https://www.gutenberg
.org/files/54691/54691-h/54691-h.htm.

Djeha and Nasreddin Hoca Variants for Children

Al-Hakkak, Ghalib. 2018. *Anecdotes de Juha: pour mieux apprendre
l'arabe*. Marmagne: Ghalib al-Hakkak.
Belamri, Rabah. 1991. *L'Âne de Djeha*. Paris: L'Harmattan.
Coué, Jean. 1993. *Djeha le malin*. Paris: Rageot.
Darwiche, Jihad and David B. 2000. *Sagesses et malices de Nasreddine,
le fou qui était sage*. Vol. 1. Paris: Albin Michel.
Darwiche, Jihad and David B. 2007. *Sagesses et malices de Nasreddine,
le fou qui était sage*. Vol. 3. Paris: Albin Michel.
Darwiche, Jihad and Pierre-Olivier Leclercq. 2003. *Sagesses et malices
de Nasreddine, le fou qui était sage*. Vol. 2. Paris: Albin Michel.
Johnson-Davies, Denys. 2005. *Goha, the Wise Fool*. New York:
Philomel Books.
Khiat, Ahmed. 2016. *Djeha: le plaisantin floué*. Saint-Denis:
Edilivre.
Zouaoui, Kamel. 2017. *Les Pas sages d'un fou: quelques aventures de
Nasredine le Hodja*. Touques: Tangerine Nights.

Secondary Sources

Aceval, Nora, ed. 2005. *Aux origines du monde: contes et traditions
d'Algérie*. Paris: Flies France.
Aceval, Nora, ed. 2011. *La Chamelle et autres contes libertins du
Maghreb*. Paris: Al Manar.
Afary, Janet and Kamran Afary. 2018. "The Rhetoric and Performance
of the Trickster Nasreddin Mullâ: Nasreddin's Guile and Dirt
Work." *Rahavard Persian Journal* 123: 24–44.
Aïtel, Fazia. 2014. *We Are Imazighen: The Development of Algerian
Berber Identity in Twentieth-Century Literature and Culture*.
Gainesville: University Press of Florida.

Alili, Rochdy. (1995) 2004. "L'Histoire de l'islam au Maghreb." In *Maghreb, peuples et civilisations*, edited by Camille Lacoste and Yves Lacoste, 131–40. Paris: La Découverte.

Amrouche, Taos Marguerite. 1966. *Le Grain magique: contes, poèmes et proverbes berbères de Kabylie*. Paris: Maspéro.

Anonymous. 1990. *The Koran*, translated by N. J. Dawood. London: Penguin Classics.

Anonymous. 2018. *The Book of the Wiles of Women*, translated by John Esten Keller. Chapel Hill: North Carolina Studies in the Romance Languages and Literatures.

Bacchilega, Cristina and Anne E. Duggan, eds. 2018. *Marvels & Tales* 32, no. 1: 10. https://digitalcommons.wayne.edu/marvels/vol32/iss1/.

Bakhtin, Mikhail M. 1984. *Rabelais and His World*. Bloomington: Indiana University Press.

Baratier, Jacques, dir. 1958. *Goha*. Tunis.

Başgöz, İlhan and Pertev Nailî Boratav. 1998. *I, Hoca Nasreddin, Never Shall I Die: A Thematic Analysis of Hoca Stories*. Bloomington: Indiana University Press.

Basset, Henri. 1920. *Essai sur la littérature des Berbères*. Algiers: Jules Carbonel. https://gallica.bnf.fr/ark:/12148/bpt6k6540849h/f183 .item.texteImage.

Basset, René. 1883. *Contes arabes: histoires des dix vizirs*. Paris: Ernest Leroux.

Basset, René. 1887. *Contes populaires berbères*. Paris: Ernest Leroux. https://gallica.bnf.fr/ark:/12148/bpt6k104452o?rk=107296;4.

Basset, René. 1897. *Nouveaux contes berbères: recueillis, traduits et annotés par René Basset*. Paris: Ernest Leroux.

Basset, René. 1903. *Contes populaires d'Afrique*. Paris: Maisonneuve et Larose.

Basset, René, trans. 1924–1926. *Mille et un contes, récits et légendes arabes*. 3 Vols. Paris: Maisonneuve et Larose. https://gallica.bnf.fr /ark:/12148/bpt6k9710607r/f26.item.

Bearman, Pery J., Thierry Bianquis, Clifford Edmund Bosworth, E. J. van Donzel, and Wolfhart Heinrichs, eds. *Encyclopaedia of Islam*, 2nd ed. Leiden: Brill. https ://referenceworks.brillonline.com /browse/encyclopaedia-of-islam-2.

Bekkay, Rhimi. 1984. *Le Personnage de Moha chez Tahar Ben Jelloun et Mejdoub dans la tradition arabo-musulmane*.

Montpellier: Mémoire de licence es-lettres, Université de Montpellier 3, Paul Valéry.

Bellagh, Mohand Améziane. 1987. "Auguste Mouliéras, *Les Fourberies de Si Djeh'a (Contes Kabyles)*." *Horizons maghrébins* 11, no. 1: 102–3.

Ben Jelloun, Tahar. (1995) 2004. "Défendre la diversité culturelle du Maghreb." In *Maghreb, peuples et civilisations*, edited by Camille Lacoste and Yves Lacoste, 96–98. Paris: La Découverte.

Ben Jelloun, Tahar. 1978. *Moha le fou, Moha le sage*. Paris: Seuil.

Benattar, S. C. 1923. *Le Bled en lumière: folklore tunisien*. Paris: Éditions Jules Tallandier. https://books.google.com/books?id=599LAAAA YAAJ&pg=PA3&hl=fr&source=gbs_selected_pages&cad=2#v=one page&q&f=false.

Berger, John. 1980. *About Looking*. New York: Pantheon Books.

Bettelheim, Bruno. 1976. *The Uses of Enchantment: The Meaning and Importance of Fairy Tales*. New York: Alfred A. Knopf.

Boudjedra, Rachid. 1972. *L'Insolation*. Paris: Denoël.

Bouhdiba, Abdelwahab. 1994. *L'Imaginaire maghrébin: étude de dix contes pour enfants*. Tunis: Cérès éditions.

Bourdieu, Pierre. 1961. *The Algerians*, translated by Alan C. M. Ross. Boston: Beacon Press.

Bourdieu, Pierre. 1977. *Algérie 60: structures économiques et structures temporelles*. Paris: Les Éditions de Minuit.

Bourdieu, Pierre. 1979. *Algeria 1960*, translated by Richard Nice. Cambridge: Cambridge University Press.

Burke, Edmund. 2014. *The Ethnographic State: France and the Invention of Moroccan Islam*. Oakland: University of California Press.

Byrnum, Joyce. 1989. "Tales of Hodja Nasreddin—The Immortal Trickster." *ETC: A Review of General Semantics* 46, no. 4: 370–74.

Chabanne, Jean-Charles, ed. 2002. *Le Comique*. Paris: Gallimard.

Cherif, Mohamed Hédi. (1995) 2004a. "L'Empreinte des appartenances sur les communautés." In *Maghreb, peuples et civilisations*, edited by Camille Lacoste and Yves Lacoste, 99–107. Paris: La Découverte.

Cherif, Mohamed Hédi. (1995) 2004b. "Les Statuts et les formes de propriété." In *Maghreb, peuples et civilisations*, edited by Camille Lacoste and Yves Lacoste, 108–17. Paris: La Découverte.

Daudet, Alphonse. (1910) 1921. *Tartarin of Tarascon and Tartarin of the Alps*, edited by Ernest Rhys. London and Toronto: J. M. Dent &

Sons and New York: E. P. Dutton & Co. https://books.google.com
/books?id=FFdoK6VfHpIC&printsec=frontcover&hl=fr&source
=gbs_ge_summary_r&cad=0#v=onepage&q&f=false.

Déjeux, Jean. 1976. "Djoha, héros de la tradition orale, dans la littérature algérienne de langue française." *Revue de l'Occident musulman
et de la Méditerranée* 22: 27–35. https://www.persee.fr/doc/remmm
_0035-1474_1976_num_22_1_1375.

Déjeux, Jean. 1978. *Djoh'a: héros de la tradition orale arabo-berbère:
hier et aujourd'hui.* Sherbrooke: Naaman.

Déjeux, Jean, ed. 1987. "Avant-propos." *Les Fourberies de Si Djeh'a:
Contes kabyles,* 7–25. Paris: La Boîte à Documents.

Déjeux, Jean. 1995. "Djoha et la nâdira." *Revue du monde musulman et
de la Méditerranée: L'humour en Orient* 77–78: 41–49. https://doi
.org/10.3406/remmm.1995.1710.

Dermenghem, Émile. 1954. *Le Culte des saints dans l'islam maghrébin.*
Paris: Gallimard.

Dib, Mohammed. 1955. *Au Café: nouvelles.* Paris: Gallimard.

Diop, Cheikh. 2005. "Mythes et symbolisation: la re-présentation
du fou au Maghreb et en Afrique noire à travers *Moha le fou,
Moha le sage* (Tahar Ben Jelloun) et *Toiles d'araignées* (Ibrahima
Ly)." In *Ajouter du monde au monde: Symboles, symbolisations,
symbolismes culturels dans les littératures francophones d'Afrique
et des Caraïbes,* edited by Frédéric Mambenga-Ylagou, 255–99.
Montpellier: Université Paul-Valéry.

Dols, Michael Walters. 1992. *Majnūn: The Madman in Medieval Islamic
Society.* Oxford: Clarendon Press.

Doutté, Edmond. 1909. *Magie et religion dans l'Afrique du Nord.*
Algiers: Adolphe Jourdan. https://gallica.bnf.fr/ark:/12148/bpt6k
82678p?rk=21459;2.

Dundes, Alan. 1989. *Folklore Matters.* Knoxville: University of
Tennessee Press.

Feraoun, Mouloud. 1960. *Les Poèmes de Si Mohand.* Paris: Minuit.

Fernandes, Ana Raquel. 2008. "Trickster." *The Greenwood Encyclopedia
of Folktales and Fairy Tales,* vol. 3, edited by Donald Haase, 992–95.
Westport: Greenwood Press.

Foucault, Michel. 1965. *Madness and Civilization: A History of Insanity
in the Age of Reason.* New York: Pantheon Books.

Galley, Micheline and Zakia Iraqui Sinaceur, eds. 1994. *Dyab, Jha, La'âba . . . le triomphe de la ruse: contes marocains du fond Colin.* Paris: Classiques africains.

Gautier, Théophile. (1845) 1865. *Loin de Paris.* Paris: Michel Lévy Frères.

Haddadou, Akli Mohand. 2000. *Le Guide de la culture berbère.* Paris: Paris-Méditerranée.

Haddawy, Husain and Muhsin Mahdi. 1990. *The Arabian Nights.* New York: W. W. Norton.

Hanoteau, Adolphe. 1867. *Poésies populaires de la Kabylie du Jurjura.* Paris: Imprimerie impériale.

Hanoteau, Adolphe and Aristide Horace Letourneux. 1872–1873. *La Kabylie et les coutumes kabyles.* Paris: Imprimerie nationale.

Irwin, Robert. 2018. *Ibn Khaldun: An Intellectual Biography.* Princeton: Princeton University Press.

Jenkins, Ronald Scott. 1994. *Subversive Laughter: The Liberating Power of Comedy.* New York: Free Press.

Jones, Christa C. 2010. "On Performative Encounters: The Portrayal of Literary Souks in North African Francophone Fiction." *Women's Studies Quarterly* 38, nos. 3–4: 185–202.

Jones, Christa C. 2012a. *Cave Culture in Maghrebi Literature: Imagining Self and Nation.* Lanham: Lexington Books.

Jones, Christa C. 2012b. "La Représentation du corps dans le hammam fictionnel maghrébin." In *Penser le corps au Maghreb,* edited by Monia Lachheb, 123–36. Paris: Karthala and Tunis: Institut de Recherche sur le Maghreb Contemporain.

Jones, Christa C. 2017. "Ecocriticism *avant la lettre*: Human-animal encounters in colonial travelogues by Gautier, Fromentin, Lorrain, Loti and Maupassant." *Studies in Travel Writing* 21, no. 3: 278–92.

Khaldun, Ibn. 1969. *The Muqaddimah: An Introduction to History,* translated by Franz Rosenthal. Princeton: Princeton University Press.

Lacoste, Yves. (1995) 2004. "Des formes très différentes de colonisation." In *Maghreb, peuples et civilisations,* edited by Camille Lacoste and Yves Lacoste, 28–29. Paris: La Découverte.

Lacoste, Yves. (1995) 2004. "Ibn Khaldoun, un grand penseur du XVe siècle." In *Maghreb, peuples et civilisations,* edited by Camille Lacoste and Yves Lacoste, 15. Paris: La Découverte.

Lacoste-Dujardin, Camille. (1995) 2004. "Structures familiales: de la grande famille aux nouvelles familles." In *Maghreb, peuples et civilisations*, edited by Camille Lacoste and Yves Lacoste, 119–25. Paris: La Découverte.

Lacoste-Dujardin, Camille. 1987. *Discrimination garçon-fille à la naissance et dans la petite enfance au Maghreb*. Paris: AECLAS.

Lacoste-Dujardin, Camille. 2003. *Le Voyage d'Idir et Djya en Kabylie: initiation à la culture kabyle*. Paris: L'Harmattan.

Lacoste-Dujardin, Camille. 2005. *Dictionnaire de la culture berbère en Kabylie*. Paris: La Découverte.

Leeming, David. 1979. "The Hodja." *Parabola: The Trickster* 4, no. 1: 84–89.

Lorcin, Patricia. (1995) 2014. *Imperial Identities: Stereotyping, Prejudice, and Race in Colonial Algeria*. Lincoln: University of Nebraska Press.

Loti, Pierre. (1914) 1929. *Morocco (Au Maroc) by Pierre Loti*, translated by W. P. Baines. London: T. Werner Lauri.

Mammeri, Mouloud. 1980. *Machaho!: contes berbères de Kabylie*. Paris: Bordas.

Marzolph, Ulrich. 1983. *Der Weise Narr Buhlūl*. Wiesbaden: Franz Steiner.

Marzolph, Ulrich. 1987. "Der Weise Narr Buhlūl in den modernen Volksliteraturen der islamischen Länder." In *Fabula* 28: 72–89. http://wwwuser.gwdg.de/~umarzol/files/06Marzolph_Buhlul.pdf.

Marzolph, Ulrich. 1991. "Zur Überlieferung der Nasreddin Hodscha-Schwänke außerhalb des türkischen Sprachraumes." In *Türkische Sprachen und Kulturen, Materialien der 1. Deutschen Turkologen-Konferenz*, edited by Ingeborg Baldauf, Klaus Kreiser, and Semih Tezcan, 275–85. Wiesbaden: Harrassowitz.

Marzolph, Ulrich. 1992. *Arabia ridens: die humoristische Kurzprosa der frühen adab-Literatur im internationalen Traditionsgeflecht*. Frankfurt am Main: Vittorio Klostermann.

Marzolph, Ulrich. 1999. "*Adab* in Transition: Creative Compilation in Nineteenth Century Print Tradition." In *Compilation and Creation in Adab and Luga: Studies in Memory of Naphtali Kinberg (1948–1997)*, edited by Albert Arazi, Joseph Sadan, and David J. Wasserstein, 161–72. Tel Aviv: Eisenbrauns. http://wwwuser.gwdg.de/~umarzol/files/42Marzolph_Adab-in-transition.pdf.

Marzolph, Ulrich. 2000. "The Qoran and Jocular Literature." *Arabica* 47: 478–87. http://wwwuser.gwdg.de/~umarzol/files/46Marzolph _Qoran-Jocular.pdf.

Marzolph, Ulrich. 2005. "Juḥā in the *Arabian Nights*." *Journal of Arabic Literature* 36, no. 3: 311–22.

Marzolph, Ulrich. 2006. "Juha." In *Medieval Islamic Civilization: An Encyclopedia*, vol. 1, edited by Josef W. Meri, 426. New York: Routledge.

Marzolph, Ulrich. 2009. *Humor in der arabischen Kultur*. Berlin: Walter de Gruyter.

Marzolph, Ulrich. 2011. "The Muslim Sense of Humor." In *Humor and Religion: Challenges and Ambiguities*, edited by Hans Geybels and Walter Van Herck, 169–87. London: Bloomsbury.

Marzolph, Ulrich. 2012. "Naṣr al-Dīn Khodja." In *The Encyclopaedia of Islam*, edited by P. Bearman, Th. Bianquis, C. E. Bosworth, E. van Donzel, and W. P. Heinrichs. 2nd ed. Leiden: Brill. http://dx.doi.org /10.1163/1573-3912_islam_SIM_5842.

Marzolph, Ulrich. 2017. "Juḥā." In *The Encyclopaedia of Islam*, edited by Kate Fleet, Gudrun Krämer, Denis Matringe, John Nawas, and Everett Rowson, 139–41. 3rd ed. Leiden: Brill.

Maupassant, Guy Henri René de. 1903. *Au Soleil, or African Wanderings. La Vie Errante or In Vagabondia*. Vol. 12. Acron: St. Dunstan Society.

Melchert, Christopher. 2015. *Hadith, Piety, and Law: Selected Studies*. Atlanta: Lockwood Press.

Micha, Alexandre, ed. 1989. *Fabliaux du Moyen Âge*. Paris: Flammarion.

Mir, Mustansir. 1991. "Humor in the Qur'ān." *Muslim World* 81, nos. 3–4: 179–93.

Mouliéras, Auguste. 1893. *Légendes et contes merveilleux de la Grande Kabylie*. Paris: Ernest Leroux. https://gallica.bnf.fr/ark:/12148/bp t6k104520h.image; http://www.berberemultimedia.fr/bibliotheque /auteurs/Moulieras_legendes_1898.pdf.

Mouliéras, Auguste. 1895–1899. *Le Maroc inconnu: 22 ans d'explorations dans cette contrée mystérieuse, de 1872 à 1893*. Paris: Joseph André.

Mouliéras, Auguste. 1965. *Traduction des légendes et contes de la Grande Kabylie recueillis par Auguste Mouliéras,* translated by Camille Lacoste. Paris: Librairie Orientaliste Paul Geuthner.

Muzi, Jean. 2003. *30 contes du Maghreb*. Paris: Castor Poche.

Nacib, Youssef. 1981. *Éléments sur la tradition orale*. Algiers: SNED.

Nacib, Youssef. 1982. *Contes algériens du Djurdjura*. Paris: Publisud.

Nacib, Youssef. 1986. *Contes de Kabylie*. Paris: Publisud.

Nacib, Youssef. 2002. *Proverbes et dictons kabyles: oralité sapientiale*. Algiers: Maison des Livres.

Ouary, Malek. 1974. *Poèmes et chants de Kabylie*. Paris: Librairie Saint-Germain-des-Prés.

Primiano, Leonard Norman. 1995. "Vernacular Religion and the Search for Method in Religious Folklife." *Western Folklore* 54, no. 1: 33–56.

Reynaud-Paligot, Carole. 2006. *La République raciale (1860–1930)*. Paris: PUF.

Richardson, Joanna. 1958. *Théophile Gautier: His Life and Times*. London: Max Reinhardt.

Rivière, Joseph. 1882. *Contes populaires de la Kabylie du Djurdjura*. Paris: Ernest Leroux.

Rosenthal, Franz. 1956. *Humor in Early Islam*. Philadelphia: University of Pennsylvania Press.

Scelles-Millie, Jeanne. 2002. *Contes mystérieux d'Afrique du nord*. Paris: Maisonneuve et Larose.

Schaeffer, Neil. 1981. *The Art of Laughter*. New York: Columbia University Press.

Schmidt, Jean-Jacques. 2005. *Le Livre de l'humour arabe*. Arles: Actes Sud.

Schnerb, Claude. 2003. *Du Rire: comique, esprit, humour*. Paris: Imago.

Servier, Jean. 1962. *Les Portes de l'année, rites et symboles: l'Algérie dans la tradition méditerranéenne*. Paris: Robert Laffont.

Sims, Martha C. and Martine Stephens. 2005. *Living Folklore: An Introduction to the Study of People and Their Traditions*. Logan: Utah State University Press.

Taïa, Abdellah. 2000. *Mon Maroc*. Paris: Séguier.

Tillion, Germaine. 1958. *Algeria: The Realities*, translated by Ronald Matthews. New York: Alfred A. Knopf.

Uther, Hans-Jörg. 2004. *The Types of International Folktales: A Classification and Bibliography, Based on the System of Antti Aarne and Stith Thompson*. 3 Vols. Helsinki: Suomalainen Tiedeakatemia, Academia Scientiarum Fennica.

Yacine, Kateb. 1975. *Mohamed, prends ta valise*. Paris: Théâtre des Bouffes du nord.

Zafrani, Haïm. (1995) 2004. "Les Juifs au Maghreb, une histoire deux fois millénaires." In *Maghreb, peuples et civilisations*, edited by Camille Lacoste and Yves Lacoste, 149–54. Paris: La Découverte.

Zarrouki, Muhammad. 1951. "Djuha (Nasr al-Din Khodja): A Study of Master of Wit in the Middle Eastern Folk-Lore." *Islamic Review* 39, no. 6: 17–19.

Zoubeida, Mameria. 2013. *Contes du terroir algérien*. Vol. 3. Algiers: Dalimen.

Index

About the Editor

Photo courtesy of the editor

Christa Catherine Jones (PhD, Washington University in St. Louis, 2006) is professor of French in the Department of World Languages and Cultures at Utah State University, where she teaches a variety of French literature and culture classes, ranging from Business French, France Today, French Culture and Civilization, Chanson and Variété Française to French and Francophone fairy tales. She is coeditor of *Algerian Filmmaker Merzak Allouache* (2017), *New Approaches to Teaching Folk and Fairy Tales* (2016), and *Women from the Maghreb* (2014) and author of *Cave Culture in Maghrebi Literature: Imagining Self and Nation* (2012). She is currently coediting *The Routledge Companion to Fairy Tales*. Her research on Maghrebian literature, music, and film has appeared in *Al-Raida*, *Contemporary*

French and Francophone Studies, Dalhousie French Studies, Expressions maghrébines, Francofonia, French Review, Jeunesse, Nouvelles Etudes Francophones, Research in African Literatures, the *Journal of North African Studies, Studies in Travel Writing, Women's Studies Quarterly,* and numerous edited collections.